Majine Masca

Five Little Martins
and
The Martin House

by
Caroline Van Buren

The Goldsmith Publishing Company
Chicago

CONTENTS

FIVE LITTLE MARTINS

AND THE MARTIN HOUSE

Five Little Martins
and
The Martin House

CHAPTER I

THE FIVE LITTLE MARTINS

THE sun shone straight into the breakfast room of the Martin House. It sparkled in the glasses of orange juice there upon the table, it glanced across the yellow and blue cloth, caressing the bowl of daffodils, it deepened the gold of the canary in his cage near the window, and it shone upon the early morning faces of the five little Martins.

It was a golden morning, it was a cheerful morning, the kind that makes one glad just to be alive. The five little Martins were very much alive as their shining eyes and gay voices told.

"Ting — a-ling — a — ling."

It was the front door bell. It seemed to say, "Hurry — hurry — hurry," — just like that.

Little Rob Martin, looking up from his oatmeal, said: "Let me go."

Mary Frances, the youngest of the five little Martins, cried: "Oh, let me go!"

Sarah Martin pushed back her chair. "Let me go."

"We're going."

It was the twins — Martie and Milton. They said it in one breath, as they always did things together.

They all went.

A boy in blue was standing before the door. In one hand he held a yellow envelope, in the other a stub of a pencil. He wore a cap pulled over his eye, and his mouth was puckered as if to whistle. He grinned as he handed the little black book to Milt, saying just one word:

"Sign."

Milton nodded. He wanted the boy to know that he knew what the little black book was for, that he knew just what to do when a telegram came. He searched for the place and wrote his name, carefully, painstakingly, while all four little Martins leaned over his shoulder to see him do it.

Telegrams were thrilling; a boy dressed in blue with a cap pulled mostly over one eye was equally so. The eyes of the five little Martins were round with questions as they went trooping back to the breakfast room carrying the yellow envelope, most importantly.

"It was a boy. He brought a telegram," Sarah

Martin told her parents. " Milt signed; the boy told him where."

" I knew," said Milt.

" Of course," Martie nodded.

Father reached for the yellow envelope and opened it. They watched him while he read what was written inside, holding their breaths and waiting.

Father glanced across the table at Mother and smiled. " The bride and groom will be with us this afternoon," he said. " They are coming in the car. This is from Bob."

Mary Frances asked all of a sudden: " Is my uncle Bob a groom? "

Martie answered: " Yes, of course, Pigeon, and our new aunt is a bride. There has to be a groom when there is a bride, you know."

Sarah interrupted (Sarah was always interrupting). " I don't see why," she told Martie. " Why can't there be just a bride? "

Martie would have gone on to explain had anyone been listening, but no one was, not even Sarah who had asked the question. Everyone was far too excited to listen to explanations. It was pleasant to receive telegrams, it made little thrills go up and down one's back; it made one feel tingly all over. It made Martie's cheeks pink; it made Mother's eyes dance; it made everything just different.

The sun peeping in at the windows called to

them: "Come along out into the garden, you five little Martins, you; come, come, come along."

So they went.

The moment that breakfast was over they went laughing and shouting out into the garden, out into the sunshine. There they found the tingly feeling still with them, making them want to romp and tumble about upon the soft grass.

Professor Wind was in the garden that morning; he was busy teaching the flowers to bow and curtsy to one another, swaying gracefully upon their long green stems. When he caught sight of the five little Martins he made straight for them, rumpling their hair and pinching their cheeks until they were red as poppies, just to show that he was glad to see them. A rough old fellow was Professor Wind, but jolly for all that.

"Hello! hello! hello!" he seemed to say. "What do you think of this as a morning? Pretty nice, isn't it?" And away he flew to set all the white curtains fluttering and billowing at the windows.

"Oh, look, look . . . our house is a ship," cried Martie, pointing.

"A galley ship with all sails set," Milt cried. "Watch out it does not sail away and never come back any more."

Rob Martin's eyes danced. "A pirate ship,"

he shouted, "a pirate ship, and I am a pirate king, I am."

"We'll sail away to search for buried treasure! Heave ho, for the pirate ship!" Milt was dancing up and down.

"No, no," said little Mary Frances shaking her head. "I won't have our house an old pirate ship, I won't. I want it to be just our house, the nicest house that ever was, with the garden and — and everything waitin' for the bride and groom, I do."

"I say hurrah for the bride and groom!" shouted her brother Milt. "Hurrah for the ice cream Mary Ann is goin' to make! Hurrah for the great, big cake I saw in the pantry!"

"Hurrah for all the good things we're going to have to eat!" yelled Rob. "Hurrah! hurrah! come on everybody, hurrah!"

The garden fairly echoed with hurrahs. Mother came to the living-room window and called to them:

"What on earth are you children doing?"

Red in the face and rather out of breath they answered her: "We are hurrahing, Mother, because of all the nice things happening. Come out, can't you, and hurrah with us?"

Their mother laughed. "I'll have to do my hurrahing in here," she told them. "I'm busy getting ready for our guests."

She went away from the window and the five

little Martins began to play. They played hard
until lunch time and as soon as that was over,
they went upstairs to dress. At three o'clock they
were all out upon the veranda in their shining
best, which was very good indeed. Father, who
had come home early from the office, took off
his glasses when he saw them, wiped them and
put them on again for another look.

"Dear me," he said. "Dear me, I don't seem
to recognize these young people at all. I am
afraid I shall have to be introduced."

"They are," Mother told him smiling, "the
five little Martins of the Martin House, all
dressed up to meet the bride and groom. Aren't
they just too splendid for words?" Then she
turned to the children and said: "Try to keep
just as you are now, my dears."

Father asked: "Isn't that rather a large order?
It will be at least another hour or so before we
can begin to expect them."

"Well then," Mother said, "keep as clean as
you possibly can."

Father looked up over his glasses.

"Listen, young folks, I've a proposal to
make. If you young Martins appear as you look
at present, at the end of the next hour" (he
took out his watch and held it up for them
to see), "I promise to stand treat all round —
in reason, of course — for anything you may
name."

"What about a basket ball court and all?" Milton asked.

"Perfectly in order," Father told him.

"Is that all of it?" Rob wanted to know.

"Not quite all."

"What's the other part?" Sarah asked quickly.

"The other part," answered their father, looking at them all so spick and span and starchy, "the other part is that if you don't keep nice, I shall expect ALL red A's on next month's report — all of you. Is it a bargain? Is my proposal accepted?"

Milt answered airily: "Shucks, that's an easy one. Who couldn't keep clean that little while I'd like to know?"

"Easy as anything," agreed his twin.

"'Course," said Sarah and little Mary Frances in one breath, while Rob added: "I'll say it's a go."

"Good," answered their father, putting his watch back in his pocket. "Very good indeed. Every man Jack of you agrees then? I've a hunch I may win out."

"Not a chance," they called back as they started down the drive toward the high stone wall which shut the Martin place from the road, from the top of which they might catch the first glimpse of their uncle's car approaching.

They were most careful to keep to the driveway and not step on the grass because of their white shoes; also they were careful in climbing the wall not to get themselves wrinkled, and to sit in a neat row along the top. They looked so nice sitting there, the girls all fluffy and dainty, the boys in white trousers with collars all stiff and starchy, and ten white shoes sticking straight out before them as white as white could be.

They made so charming a picture that the sun, who couldn't remember seeing them in anything save playsuits in ever so long, came close to have a good look at them. Down it shone upon the five uncovered heads, gently it crept up to kiss the backs of five little necks, with warmth and thoroughness, until they began to feel slightly uncomfortable sitting there, and to wiggle a little.

Now if the sun hadn't been so charmed with the appearance of the five little Martins that it suddenly decided to become a member of the watching party; if, let us say, that friendly old fellow, the sun, had stayed behind some nice, fluffy cloud and contented himself with just peeping out now and then, all might have gone well.

Perhaps it isn't altogether fair to blame the sun for what happened; still the sun was certainly mixed up in it a good deal, for was it not the kindly attentions of the sun that made the children squirm and wish it wasn't quite so hot on the wall? Didn't the sun make little beads of perspiration stand upon their lips and under their eyes? Wasn't it the sun, too, that woke up that fat caterpillar who had been sleeping snugly on a leaf, well out of harm's way, and who now decided, since it was such a fine afternoon, to get up and go for a stroll? As luck would have it, Martie's dress was the place he selected to take his stroll upon.

Now if there was one thing on earth that Martie Martin was afraid of, that thing was a caterpillar. Sarah and even Mary Frances didn't mind them much, but Martie disliked them very much indeed. So when Milton remarked, with a wicked light in his eye, " Old dear, there's a nice, fat caterpillar on your dress," she gave a scream, just as her twin was sure she would.

Yes, Milt was all prepared for the scream, but what he wasn't prepared for was Martie's sliding straight down the wall to land in the midst of the rich earth their mother had had placed there about her rose vines. In a moment her pure, white shoes were a total wreck. An awfully queer look came over her twin's face.

" Oh, I say," he cried, and he let himself go right down into the black earth beside her. Martie refused, however, even to glance his way and walked off toward the meadow, humming a little tune just to make him think she didn't care, while the rest of them sat and stared in consternation. It had all been so sudden it took their breath away.

"Shucks," exclaimed Milton, his face brick red even up to the roots of his hair. "I'm going down to the pond," he added briefly.

"Hold on," Rob called, "I'm going with you, it's too hot sitting here."

Sarah and Mary Frances were left alone upon the wall (unless you count the sun which was still there); the caterpillar had gone, they knew not where.

"Let's go too," Mary Frances suggested. "I'll burn up if we stay here."

Sarah answered: "It's heaps safer to stay where we are."

"I can't help it," was the answer. "I'm going."

"Then I guess I will too," Sarah said, sighing, "but it's takin' a dreadful risk, Pigeon."

They stood up on the wall and managed to jump clear of the earth about the vines below. Then away they went across the meadow in the direction of the pond. There they found Martie searching the shore for bluebells. They saw at once by the tilt of her chin that she had not as yet forgiven her twin. The two boys were sitting in the little flat-bottomed boat which their father had had built for them, and which he had christened the "Kiddie Kar" because, as he laughingly said, it was the property of all five kiddies.

Rob called out as the two little girls joined them: "Hop in, folks, and let's take a row about." He shouted to Martie too, but she only answered: "No thanks."

They saw Milton steal a look at her and they knew that he was feeling pretty badly about the whole thing. " I tell you what," he yelled, "let's all of us get in and row down to the bridge . . . what say? "

The four little Martins — for even Martie turned at this — stared at their brother as though they couldn't have heard aright. This thing that he was proposing so calmly was something that they had never in all their lives dreamed of doing. The very idea took their breath away. Go on the river? Row the " Kiddie Kar " down to the bridge? What was Milt thinking of?

The pond was their especial playground; they had been raised upon it as well as in it; they had always spent a part of each day there. In its shallow waters they had bathed and fished and waded countless times. Upon its bank they had made mud-pies days without end. The pond was theirs to do with as they saw fit; it was both friend and playmate to them all; but the river was a very different matter.

In order to reach the bridge Milt was speaking of they would be obliged to go down the river for about a mile, and the river, as they well knew, was both deep and treacherous. The current was swift, and there were great holes about which the water eddied terrifyingly. They knew as well as they knew anything that they had not the slightest business on the river; also they knew why Milton had suggested this wild plan. He was trying to think of a way to get Martie to join them. He knew that the spirit of adventure was strong in her and that it might draw her when nothing else would. It was a well-known fact that neither twin was happy away from the other. Milt was sorry and heartily desired to make up; Martie wanted to make up, too; but she felt that her mischievous twin needed to suffer longer for his sins; therefore she refused with a toss of her head.

"Don't believe I care to go in the boat. I'll walk along the bank and look out for bluebells; I'll meet you at the bridge."

All the zest of the undertaking was gone for Milton at her refusal, but, having been the one to suggest it, he felt that he must stand by his idea and get what fun he could out of it. It was his duty to see it through; he could not back out now even if he wanted to. "All aboard!" he called, giving a hasty look at the resolute set of his twin's back. Poor Milt! How he wished that caterpillar had never been born!

The twins were like two bright stars that twinkled side by side; like stars they dazzled one who saw them for the first time; made one blink and gasp a little, take a long look and say to their mother if she were anywhere around: "What unusual children, Mrs. Martin!" And their mother would answer smiling: "Thank you, yes, I think all of my children unusual; but that is a failing common to all mothers, I believe."

They were all good to look at, those five, jolly little Martins; they had the dearest faces in the world and the merriest eyes; even serious little Mary Frances had a way of smiling at you that made you want to pick her up and give her a hug. Their mother and father were exceedingly proud of them, of their bright minds, of their healthy little bodies, of their nice manners; proud of them through and through.

At this very moment their uncle Bob was saying to their new aunt: "You'll like 'em a lot, they are jolly little beggars."

"I can't wait to see them," she answered, little knowing how short a time it would be before she did see them, or under what circumstances it would be.

"Sit tight, everybody," called Milton.

They had come to the place where the pond ceased to be just a peaceful little pond and became instead a stream which, in a very short time, would empty into the great rushing river itself. The "Kiddie Kar" seemed almost to pause in its rapid rate as though to say: "Don't do it! Listen to me; be good children; turn back while there is a chance — back where we belong!"

It was no use. They had made up their minds

to be naughty; so away they went to where danger awaited them in the deep, green waters of the river.

"Say, this is something like," Rob cried, and the others agreed with him, although little Mary Frances, grasping the sides of the boat tightly, tried not to look at the water that rushed by on either side, carrying their small craft along as though it were only a leaf cast there by the wind which might at any moment disappear altogether. Stealing a glance at Sarah she felt that Sarah also would not be sorry when they reached the bridge and their mad trip was over.

High up there on the bank they could see Martie trudging along. She had taken the short cut to the river through the woods and was well on her way to the bridge. She shouted to them and waved her hand, and they shouted and waved back. She pointed to where a clump of bluebells grew along the edge of the cliff.

Suddenly they saw it all just as one sees a picture that is flashed upon the screen — Martie high above them there on the cliff, reaching for the bluebells, one moment; the next slipping, slipping, down — down — down that dreadful bank; clutching at things to save herself, and then the black waters closing over her bright head!

For one agonizing moment they sat there in the boat unable to move or speak; just looking at the place where Martie had disappeared. Then there was a splash, the " Kiddie Kar " rocked violently as though it were about to turn over; then it righted itself, and they saw that Milton was in the water, swimming, swimming toward his twin, who had come up and was fighting bravely.

"Hold hard, Martie!" they heard him call. " I'm coming, Martie! I'm coming! Don't give up, Martie, keep fighting," and in another moment the two shining heads were side by side, while the swift current carried them rapidly down stream.

Another picture seemed to flash, as it were, before their frightened eyes. Out upon the bridge, not far away now, a big, red automobile shot and stopped. Two people stood up in the car pointing, then a man sprang out and began to climb hastily out upon the steel girders that held up the bridge; balancing there with one hand, while with the other he waited to grasp the two children whom the water was sweeping on toward him. Would they come near enough for him to reach them? Or would they be carried far out of reach of his hand? The water under the bridge was racing swiftly along; what if that outstretched hand should fail? The children asked themselves the question silently, white faced, trembling. For a moment they closed their eyes to shut out the dreadful picture; when they opened them again there was another figure there on the bridge.

A slight figure in a blue dress had leaped from the car and in her hands they saw that she carried a heavy robe; she ran to the other side of the bridge then, wrapping the robe about the railing, she seemed to brace herself to hold it there as she tossed the other end into the water.

The boy and girl in the river were being carried out of reach of the man's extended hand. The one hope remaining was the robe. Would they, Oh, could they, grasp it?

" Catch! catch hold! "

A clear voice rang out above the noise of the rushing water. " Oh, dear God, please, please let them! " prayed the children watching.

" Catch! catch hold! "

With all the strength of which he was capable Milton snatched at the heavy robe; snatched and missed, and snatched again, with one hand, while with the other he clung to his twin for the few seconds which it took the man upon the supports of the bridge to climb out to him, to drag them up, Martie first and then Milt, up, up to safety.

In another moment the "Kiddie Kar" was bumping against the sides of the bridge with its load of frightened children, and a white-faced, shaky Rob was making fast the rope. Then the children scrambled silently out of the boat, and the adventure was over.

Their uncle Bob — for it was the bride and groom who had saved the twins — gave one long look. Then, turning to the lady, who was down on her knees rubbing Martie's arms and face, he said, with a wave of his hand:

"My dear, allow me to introduce you to your nieces and nephews, the five little Martins. For the love of Mike, will you children tell me what it was that you were trying to put over this time?"

"We were trying to surprise you," Sarah said.

"Well," he answered, "you did it. You were successful. You gave me the surprise of my life — only don't do it again, I beg of you. One surprise like this is quite enough to last a life time. Come on and meet your aunt Bettina."

The new aunt was smiling at them while the twins, limp and dazed, lay on the floor of the bridge with their eyes closed. Looking at them uncle Bob said quickly: "We'd better get these two home and into something dry as soon as possible. Do you feel up to traveling now, young folks?"

He wrapped Martie in the bride's coat, and taking her in his arms he carried her to where the big car waited. Then he came back, picked up Milton and placed him beside his sister, after which he tucked him up in his own coat.

"Take things easy, you two, lie still and we'll have you home in a jiffy now," he told them kindly. " Tumble in quickly, the rest of you, and let's get going."

Martie opened her eyes just as they moved off and gave one swift glance at the river. " Please, uncle Bob, take us away," she managed to whisper.

A hand stole out of the sleeve of her uncle Bob's coat and along the seat until it found and clasped her own — clasped it tightly. All was at peace once more between the twins. All the crossness had been washed away back there in those dreadful waters where they had struggled together.

Such wretched little Martins as they were, to be sure; such bedraggled, woe-begone creatures! Who ever would have recognized them as the spick and span little people who had sat upon the old stone wall so short a time ago, so very, very sure of themselves?

Sarah said sadly, as the car rolled away: " It looks very much as if Father had won the wager."

A pink hair ribbon, floating upon the surface of the water, seemed to answer emphatically: " It does."

CHAPTER II

Red A's

(The five little Martins pay the piper)

FATHER was nice about it; but then Father was nice about everything. He came into the room where Mother was helping the twins off with their wet garments and into something dry, and said, with a disappointed look:

"So you are not to be trusted after all." He had heard the story from their uncle Bob a few minutes before.

The other little Martins were in the next room and Father was standing in the doorway. There was a long moment when they wished that the floor might open and drop them all through somewhere else — anywhere away from that reproachful look in Father's eyes.

"But, Father," began Rob, "you never told us not to go on the river."

"No," was the answer. "No, I never did. I never thought it necessary. I trusted to your own good sense. I knew that you knew very well, without being told, that you would have been forbidden to go there if you had asked. I thought that would be enough. It seems that I was mistaken. I think I had better begin now to lay down rules — thou shalt and thou shalt not."

"No, Father, please don't do that."

It was little Mary Frances who spoke. "Rules are just horrid; just because they are rules you want right off to smash them; you know you do."

Father looked at her and asked: "How then, daughter, am I to keep five foolish young people from endangering five very precious lives whenever the notion strikes them? What would you suggest?"

"That you give 'em another chance," she answered at once, "before you begin making rules. Next time we'll stop and think; truly we will." Their father was silent for a moment, then he said: "Very well, I will; trusting that you will stop and think things out before you rush ahead. Suppose," he crossed to the twins and placed an arm about each until they rested just above his heart, "suppose that because of a piece of dangerous mischief, two of you were missing now?"

It was not until later that he spoke of the red A's and of their bargain.

Mother gave the twins something hot to drink and put them to bed until dinner time; the others she sent to the bath rooms to make themselves presentable all over again. When the new aunt came in there were the twins tucked up in Mother's big bed and looking as solemn as owls.

"Do you feel like having a visit?" she asked. "Is there anything that I can do for you?"

Milt grinned. "It seems to me," he said, "you've done a good deal for us already. We are no end grateful to you and uncle Bob. If it hadn't been for you—" he paused, unable to go on.

"Don't!"

Martie leaned back on the pillow and closed her eyes as though to shut out the picture of that dreadful, rushing river. "We'll always love you for what you did," she said shyly. "Always."

Her twin added: "You bet we will!"

"I'm glad we happened along," was the answer, with a smile which told them just how glad she really was. "Now, if you feel up to talking, suppose you tell me about everybody. I know that you are the twins, but which of you comes next?"

"Rob," they told her. "Then Sarah, and last of all, Pigeon."

"Not really Pigeon of course?"

"Oh, no, Mary Frances, although almost everybody calls her Pigeon."

"How on earth did she happen to be called that?"

Martie explained: "Well you see it was this way. When she was just a tiny thing she used to adore to climb on Father's lap and cuddle down deep, with her face against his arm, while he read his paper in the evening. Father said all the time that she was there she made queer little cooing

sounds which reminded him of the baby pigeons
on the roof; and so he began to call her Pigeon-
bird and then just Pigeon. We all took it up —
that is, all but Mother, who doesn't like nick-
names. Mother says it's a perfect shame to go
and spoil a perfectly good name like Mary Frances (she is named for our two grandmothers).
Still Pigeon seems to suit her somehow."

"Tomorrow," volunteered Milton, "we'll take
you all round the place and show you everything.
Say, do you like pets?"

"Oh, ever so much! . . . have you a dog?"

"Two. Major belongs to us, and Sallie, down
at the barn, is Father's hunting dog. We've a
pony named Dandy, and lots of rabbits and a
cat."

"Oh, my, such a superior cat," Martie broke
in. "Her name is Cora, and really you would
suppose, by the way she acts, that she owns the
place. Nothing is too good for Miss Cora, no
indeed! She takes her nap upon Mother's best
silk comfort, she delights in tangling all the
threads in the sewing basket when she sees fit,
and the softest chair in the whole house she
claims as if it were hers by right."

Bettina laughed. "I can't wait to see this
wonderful Cora," she said.

"Oh, you'll see her fast enough," Milton answered. "She's likely to fly in at the window and
land in your lap. She doesn't wait to be properly

introduced, not Cora. Major, now, stands on ceremony. I say, you'll love Major — we all do — but Cora isn't that kind. We don't any of us exactly love Cora, but we do think her pretty splendid on the whole; she's so fearless — never afraid of anything, you know."

"Tell me about your pony. I had one of my own once that I loved dearly."

"You can't help loving little Dandy," Martie told her. "He's a perfect dear. On cold mornings when there is a snap in the air, there's no holding him in, and still he's as gentle as a lamb. Pigeon rides him everywhere, sometimes without saddle or bridle. Everybody has a kind word for Dandy. Even Mary Ann, who isn't fond of pets, is good to Dandy."

"Who is Mary Ann? Is she another pet?"

The twins laughed. "Not much, she isn't; but she's a very important member of the household, Mother says. She's our cook!"

"Then I should say that she was important."

"Did you know," Martie asked, "that we had made a wager with Father? It was this afternoon, after we had dressed to wait for you and uncle Bob to come; and now we've lost. So we have to make all red A's on our reports at school. You see we promised; so, of course, we have to."

She nodded. "Of course. Tough luck though, isn't it?"

" I'll tell the world it is!" Milt gave the bed-clothes a kick.

" It was so silly of us," said his twin with a sigh.

In the days to come, the five little Martins began to realize just what a task they had before them if they were to keep their end of the bargain. They felt that they owed it to their father to keep it, for they knew that if it had been the other way around he would have carried out his part of the bargain. So they had to do the best that they could.

Even the cocksure twins began to lose something of their cocksureness as the days went by, while as for the other three, they carried about with them a look that said as plain as words: "We're up against it; but we're trying hard " — as indeed they were. They were perfectly aware that this last piece of mischief had hurt their father more than he had told them, and they all wanted to do something very special to make him proud of them. With might and main the five little Martins went after the making of those red A's.

Sarah lived with her speller near at hand; she even slept with it under her pillow. The first thing in the morning she sat up in bed and began the day by wrestling with words like " separate," " Mississippi," " Cincinnati," " extraordinary," and the like. Pigeon's stumbling block was arithmetic; sums just wouldn't come right for her. Sarah could be heard asking, in a voice as much like the teacher's as possible: " Wake up, Mary Frances Martin, and tell me at once what five times seven is? "

Dolefully would come the reply in a sleepy voice: " Oh, dear, Sarah! why do you have to go and remind me of that dreadful number work the first thing in the morning? Why do you? "

" The morning is the best time, my child," Sarah would reply. " You are fresh then. Now sit right up and begin, or I'll wash your face for you. My goodness gracious, Mary Frances, don't look so stupid! "

It was Martie who found her small sister curled up under the table in the den one afternoon weeping her heart out because of the utter impossibility of mastering the eighth table. " Don't cry, darling," coaxed Martie. " Here's a molasses cookie; take a bite, it's good. Mary Ann is making heaps of them in the kitchen. Come on out and we'll beg her for some."

" I say, we've got to do something about it," Martie told the others later.

They were all in what they called the " end room," a room off the old kitchen which, in their grandfather's time, had been known as the " summer kitchen." It was the place in which they kept all the things that were too dilapidated to be carried into the house and were yet dear to their hearts. The end room was filled with odds and ends of disused furniture, broken toys, the children's garden tools, and a trunk of dress-up things for rainy days. It was a favorite gathering place. They were there now when Martie told them that something had to be done to help Pigeon master the tables.

"She's just miserable, and it seems to me there ought to be something we could do to help. We're older, you know, so it's up to us to find a way, somehow."

"Poor old Pigeon!" Rob was busy examining an old fishing rod. "I wish to goodness I knew of something to do, but I don't."

"I tell you what," Milt spoke from the top of the dusty little organ where he sat swinging his legs. "We'll put on our thinking caps, and we'll think like a house afire from now till this time tomorrow, then we'll meet here and see who has thought up a plan to make those tables easy for Pigeon — what do you say to that?"

Sarah answered. "I've thought and thought till my head's almost bursting and haven't found a thing worth while. Oh, dear! what with bothering over Pigeon and tryin' to swallow the whole speller at once I go plumb batty at times."

Milt swung himself down. "Well, so long," he told them. "Come along, Rob, let's go play ball."

The two brothers went out and Milt called back: "Think hard everybody. Tomorrow's the

day. We'll see just what each old bean has been
able to put out — good luck."

Sarah went off to feed her rabbit and Martie,
left alone, sat there before the little old neglected
organ (once the property of her great-aunt
Martha). Her fingers touched the yellow keys,
stiff and out of tune. Her thoughts strayed here
and there as she glanced about the shadowy,
silent room. She began to play a little, picking out
a simple tune, one of the first exercises she had
ever learned; and the little organ gave back a
mournful sound. Martie's thoughts were not on
what she was doing, they were on the troublesome
problem of her little sister's work. Pigeon must
make those red A's; she must! Between them
they would surely find a way to help.

"Eight times three," she found herself saying.
"Eight times three are twenty-four! Eight times
four are thirty-two!" She was keeping time with
the music almost without knowing it. "Eight
times five are — "

She leaned over the little organ; two bright
spots of crimson flamed her cheeks; her breath
came quickly; she was making a song.

It was growing dark in the room; long shadows
were stealing across the floor, turning the end
room into a place of mystery. Outside she could
hear the boys romping on the lawn with old
Major, and Major's delighted barks.

"Here, Major! here, Major! Find him, old

boy! Find him, Major!" Then Sarah's voice: "Rob! Milt! Mother says you're to come in and get washed. It's almost time for Father to come." Away off somewhere Pigeon was calling for her: "Martie! Martie! Where are you, Martie? Has anyone seen Martie?" Still she sat there making her little song; the song which was going to make things easier for her small sister. The rusty little organ began to yield softer notes under her fingers. Oh, it was fun! She didn't want to leave even though it was so dark that she could scarcely see the keys. Twilight was giving place to night, and it was quiet outside. The children had gone in. She must go in too, but she didn't want to. She was making a song; she was making a song.

They met, as they had agreed, the next afternoon in the end room. Pigeon had gone over to play with her friend Myrtle, so that there was nothing to fear from her. She would not come bursting in to know what their conference was all about, as otherwise she might have done.

Milt, the self-appointed chairman, opened the meeting. "I say, who's thought up a way to help things along? Whoever has, let him now proceed to speak, or forever after keep quiet. Well, we'll hear what Mistress Sarah has to say for herself. . . . Rise and speak!"

Sarah rose obediently but it was not to throw much light on the matter: "I've thought and thought till my head aches," she told them. "And

I just can't think of a single thing. This morning I tried Pigeon on the eighth table and she didn't know as much as she did yesterday."

"Bad — very bad." The chairman cleared his throat and looked solemn. "Well now, we'll hear what old man Martin over there has to say."

"I haven't got a thing to say," Rob shook his head. "To save my life I can't think up a way to go pokin' things into a person's head. How'd it do to make'm for her, all those tables, in different kinds of crayons? Maybe that would help."

The chairman was doubtful. "Yes, and s'pose it don't? We haven't got all the time there is, you know. Days are passing, time is getting short. Every day we are creeping up closer to the moment for those reports to come out. What we have to do, we have to do quick; let me tell you that, folks."

"If you don't like that let's hear what you have to say for yourself," challenged Rob.

"I haven't a thing."

"Then don't ask me."

"I won't. I'll ask Martie. This committee will now proceed to hear from Mistress Martie Martin. The rest of us having proven ourselves dumbbells, let's hope that she may be able to cast some light upon a most desperate situation. Mistress Martie has the floor; you folks be quiet!"

Mistress Martie rose to her feet with a quick, little, nervous laugh. "I don't know what any of

you will think," she said. " Maybe you'll call me
a dumb-bell too; but I believe — I'm almost sure
— that I have a way of helping Pigeon."

There were cries of " Bully for you! " " Let's
hear it! " " One old bean is working in this bunch
anyway! " " Go ahead! hurry and tell us! "

" I'll show you," she told them. " Get down off
the organ, please, Milt, and don't any of you
dare laugh until I'm through; — promise! "

" We promise! Shoot! "

" Well then," Martie explained as she seated
herself at the little old organ, " I thought it out
yesterday after you had gone and I was sitting
here just making sounds on the organ. I had the
tables in my mind because we had just been talking about them, and the first thing I knew, there
I was, trying to put them into a song, to the tune
of 'Yankee Doodle,' you know. Now if you'll
listen I'll show you."

She began to play; the keys were less stiff and
the sound they produced was more like music.
She sang softly through the first table, looking
up at them smiling, half afraid that they were
going to make fun of her efforts; but they did
not. Before she had come to the end of the second
table they were singing with her and on the fourth
table they were shouting lustily, led by the old
organ, which really seemed to be enjoying itself
immensely.

" Gee, Martie, old horse, but I'm no end proud

of you," Milt declared pounding her on the back.

" And you really think — "

" 'Course we do," Rob interrupted. " Pigeon learns the longest kind of verses without any trouble. She'll eat this up."

" Yes," cried Sarah. " She will. We'll sing them together till she gets it all down pat. I say, Martie, do you know, I think you're rather splendid to have worked it all out, I do."

" How can she help from being? I'd like to know. Isn't she my twin? " grinned Milton. " Now all together; let's have a go with the eighth before this meeting breaks up. When shall we break the good news to Pigeon? "

" Not just yet," Martie cautioned. " Not till we can do a little better; say after another re-hearsal. We want her to take to the idea right off."

" All right," agreed her twin. " Tomorrow's Saturday; no old school to bother about. We'll have barrels of time to get the thing down pat. We'll meet in here right after breakfast and work on 'em. I haven't a thing to do till after lunch; then I've a date to play basket ball with some of the bunch. Listen, everybody, tomorrow's our last rehearsal before we let Pigeon in."

That Saturday morning little Mary Frances Martin sat upon the steps of the veranda idly watching Major, who lay in the sunshine con-tentedly chewing a bone. Her thoughts were running in this wise: "I wish maybe that I were a dog, a nice dog like Major, with nothing to do but lie in the sun all day long if I chose. Nothing to bother my head about — no old tiresome tables to learn. How nice it would be."

Over there by that clump of verbena there hovered a yellow butterfly; a tiny sparrow flew about on the grass, cocking his head on one side and hopping gaily about. Major glanced up from the bone he was chewing to give a low growl, and away he flew only to return in a moment and perch upon the lowest limb of a cedar tree, watching Major with bright black eyes. Through the hollyhocks there came gliding a jet ball that shone like satin in the sunlight. It was Cora, walking daintily, pretending not to see the sparrow, advancing with little, mincing steps.

"Oh, sakes alive!" thought Pigeon, "Cora is after that poor little bird. Come back, Cora, you bad thing!" she cried. "Shoo! Fly away, little bird."

She clapped her hands and the sparrow lifted his wings and flew to such a height that Cora could not catch him. She stalked indignantly away, her tail high in the air, and the last the little girl saw of her she was walking the white lattice fence, disdainfully unaware of Major's presence, or of his warning growl. "You can't frighten me," her whole attitude seemed to say; "so why waste time in trying, old thing?"

"Pigeon!" Sarah burst out of the door behind her and caught hold of her arm. "Don't you worry — everything's going to be all right, you'll see."

After dinner that evening Sarah slipped her hand into Pigeon's: "Come along with me," she whispered. "Don't say anything — just come." Her tone was heavy with mystery.

"Where?" asked Pigeon. "Where are we going?"

"Out in the end room; the others are there."

"The end room at night!"

"Yes, it's all right; the boys have their flash lights. Don't let Mary Ann know where we are going; she's sure to make a fuss."

"Is it a secret society, Sarah?" breathed Pigeon beginning to feel excited. "Is that what it is?"

"No, not exactly. Don't ask questions. You'll know soon enough."

They scudded past the kitchen when Mary Ann had her back turned; and went quickly and silently down the back steps and out to where there came a faint light from the end room. The door was shut, but when Sarah rapped three times, pausing between each rap, it opened slowly and Rob stuck his head out.

"Oh, it's you, is it? Come on in. Shut the door tight; we don't want old Mary Ann seeing the light and nosing about to spoil things."

The end room was a strange, weird place in the wavering light from the two flash lights that the boys carried; very different from what it was in the day time. In the day time an old bureau was just an old bureau standing there against the wall; now it might have been anything. Pigeon's own cast-aside high chair might have been any one of a dozen strange unfamiliar objects looming in the gloom. Martie and Sarah in their light clothes resembled huge gray moths, and the two boys were black bats with white faces.

Milton, holding the light high so that it cast a round circle upon the ceiling, while he himself was in the shadow, came forward and spoke majestically: " Sit you down here, Mistress Pigeon, and keep very, very still."

" I can't. I'm crazy to know what it's about."

" All in due time, Mistress Pigeon; calm yourself," went on the solemn voice.

" How long must I wait? "

" Oh, sit down, as Milt tells you, Pigeon, and be quiet." Sarah tugged at her arm, and pulled her down upon a rickety bench near the door.

" You talk too much, Mistress Pigeon." The chairman's voice rang sternly. " It behooves you to sit down and be quiet, and in due time you will be told all about everything."

" All right; but I do wish you'd hurry and tell me now. I'm dying to know what it's all about."

" It's about you."

" About me? "

The chairman seemed to tower nearly up to the ceiling in the light which moved here and there. " About you, Mistress Mary — Frances — Pigeon — Martin, about you. We are gathered together here tonight in this secret place, because of you — to help you."

" To help me? To help me do what? "

" To help you make red A's," was the answer. " To help you with the multiplication tables. We've found a way to make 'em easy as anything. It was Mistress Martie who thought it up. Now just you sit still and listen to this. Ready? " he asked.

" Ready," was the answer.

Martie sat at the organ, the others came and stood about her, she bent over the keys with a little fluttering motion of her hands, then she began to play and sing, the rest joining with her. They were all singing; what was this they were singing?

Pigeon, disregarding the injunction to sit still, was on her feet. She even forgot herself so far as to grasp the exalted chairman's arm: " Oh, I say! Oh, I say, how'd you ever, ever do it? How did you? Learn 'em now? Of course I can; how perfectly scrumptious! Of course I can learn every one; anybody could now. Oh! O-h-h! "

The day dawned; the fatal day, as they say in books. The five little Martins felt it to be a very fatal day indeed. Five thin white envelopes stood in a line upon the mantel in the living room . . . five busy minds were asking themselves: "Oh, I wonder! Have I done it? Will there be all red A's in mine?"

Save for the ticking of the clock and the whispering of the fire not a sound broke the stillness as their father took down, one by one, those envelopes; and, taking out the card within, read what was written thereon.

"Crick! crick!" murmured the fire gently.

"Tick! tock!" said the clock.

"Children!"

Father held out his hands to them all without saying a word more. There was no need to; they understood; they knew; they had made good! Such a rejoicing! The big room rang with cheers. They danced, they pranced, they whirled about their father, laughing, shouting, all talking at once.

"Crick! crick!" snapped the fire. "Did you ever in all your life see such noisy children?"

"Tick! tock!" answered the clock. "I can't say that I ever did."

"I think I'll just go out," the fire hissed, "until they're through."

"Oh, I wouldn't," the clock ticked; and added to the general din by striking as loud as it could.

"Where's Mother?" Father always asked when anything nice happened: "Where's Mother?"

"Here I am," she answered from the doorway, "and as proud as a peacock."

With one grand rush they made for her and catching hold of her hands began to prance wildly about. "Wait!" she cried out. "If you will be still a moment and listen I think you may like what I have to say."

There was instant quiet.

"How pleasant!" the fire murmured.

Mother told them: "Mary Ann and I have been busy in the kitchen — you see I was so sure of you. Go and see what you can find."

They went. They found a big, white frosted cake with a red A upon the top; there was also a tall, glass pitcher of lemonade. Later when they were seated about the dining-room table, and Mother had cut the cake, their father rose and faced them with his glass of lemonade held high in his hand.

"I give you," he said, smiling, "the five little Martins — on their mettle."

"Here's to red A's," Milton cried, bobbing up. "They're pretty fine once they're made; but gee whiz! the making!"

"Here's to English!" Martie nodded impressively. "For once I've got the better of it."

"And words!" exclaimed Sarah. "Long ones,

short ones, big ones, and little one-syllable words
— all kinds. I like 'em a lot better than I did."

" And old geography ! " Rob held his glass high.

" And — and multiplication tables! " Pigeon
almost turned over her glass in her hurry to get
to her feet. Her eyes were shining like two bright
lamps in a window. " I can sing them every one,
I can."

" Pigeon," Sarah whispered, as they lay side by
side in their little beds that night. " Do you s'pose,
Pigeon, that if we'd died and gone straight to
heaven we could feel any happier than we do
right this minute? "

After a minute's thought came the answer:
" No, Sarah, no; I don't believe we could."

CHAPTER III

ANNETTE

L ISTEN, children; Martie especially."

Mrs. Martin glanced up from the letter she had been reading, " Here is something of interest to you. This letter is from a very old friend of mine, Mrs. Curtis. You know the old Curtis place, The Oaks, on the way to town? Mrs. Curtis used to live there, and now she is sending her little granddaughter there for several weeks."

"Why is she sending her? " Martie asked interestedly. " Isn't she coming too, Mother? "

"No," her mother answered. "Alice Curtis is an invalid and cannot take the long trip. Listen and I will read you what she says about it."

" ' I am sending little Annette to The Oaks for a few weeks in hopes that the sunshine and milder climate may bring the roses back to her cheeks. Annette, who has never been a strong child, is recovering from a fall she had while skating some time ago. She fell and fractured her leg just above the knee, and she is still on crutches. Besides the sunshine of the old place I am counting — perhaps even more — on the companionship of your children to help make Annette well. Having children to play with will be a real treat to her, and I am going to ask that, as a favor to me, you will ask the children to go as often as they can while she is there. I am sorry that I cannot accompany the child. As it is I am sending a person who is a sort of nurse-housekeeper, and who seems devoted to Annette. They will arrive the latter part of the week.'

" I believe that's about all that will interest you in the letter. The little girl, Annette, is very near Martie's age."

" I'll go right off to see her," Martie announced, nodding her curly head, and Sarah asked: "Why doesn't her mother come with her? "

"Both of Annette's parents are dead," her mother answered. " She has lived with her grandmother ever since she was a small child. We must have her often at the Martin House and do what we can to make her stay a pleasant one."

The old Curtis place became from that moment of interest to the five Martin children. Hitherto it had seemed a place asleep, now suddenly it became awake over night. Blinds were opened, shades went up, a gardener came and cut the grass, the whole place took on an air of expectation as though waiting for something nice to happen. It had been decided that Martie was to go alone for the first visit, after which they might all ride over as often as they pleased.

So, dressed in her very best, and looking as

sweet as a rose, Martie set forth in the pony cart escorted by the four other little Martins, some on wheels, some in the cart beside her, to make the first call at The Oaks.

"Now, Martie, listen," Sarah instructed. "Be sure to remember every single little thing that happens, so you can tell us. It's just simply thrilly having a little, new girl come. I'm absolutely dying to know 'xactly what she looks like and all that."

"I'll tell you everything," her sister promised faithfully.

"Be sure and see how many dolls she has," Pigeon commanded.

"Rats! Who cares 'bout old dolls?" Rob was scornful as he coasted down the hill, feet upon the handle bars. "Ask her 'bout her pets; maybe she brought a dog with her."

"Maybe a monkey," Milt suggested. "Or a parrot."

"Oh, I wonder if she did!" Sarah's eyes were sparkling as she turned to Martie. "Find out everything that's interesting, every single thing; do. We'll ride on to the village and do our shopping, then we'll come back and stop for you. Mother said that would be plenty long for the first time."

Pigeon reminded her sister: "Don't forget you are to ask her to come day after tomorrow, 'cause it's Saturday, and spend the day with us."

" I'll remember," Martie answered, patting her nicely folded handkerchief and sitting very straight, so as not to wrinkle her dress.

" Say, don't you feel queer, Martie, going all by yourself? "

" Ye — s, a little."

" Now don't go and get cold feet at the last moment," her twin directed. " We'll be waiting when you come out; and for pity's sake don't make it long."

" No, I won't," Martie answered as they brought the pony cart to a stop outside the high hedge which cut off all save a glimpse or two of the big house behind it. She climbed down with an anxious, " Do I look all right, Sarah? Is my dress much rumpled? Oh, dear, I've dropped my handkerchief again! "

" Here 'tis," Milt swooped from his wheel and presented it to her. " Trot along in, old thing, and good luck."

They were off, leaving Martie to go up the walk and ring the bell, feeling rather deserted and somewhat bashful. What would they find to talk about? Suppose they did not find anything; suppose they just sat still and looked at each other. Suppose they couldn't think of a single thing to say; wouldn't it be terrible? Now if only Milt were with her, Milt who was never at a loss for something to say. Oh, dear, there was no help for it now. Five minutes later she was back upon the road, gazing on the long, sunshiny stretch ahead of her and wondering what on earth she had better do to pass the time. How different the visit had turned out from what she had expected; how disappointed they would all be. She decided to walk on and meet them.

Trudging along through the dust and heat of the afternoon, Martie was feeling pretty miserable when she saw them coming. Dan at a brisk trot toward his stable and supper, the two boys upon their bicycles; such a jolly, happy crowd, having such a good time. It was Milt who first caught sight of her, and almost tumbled from his seat in amazement.

"Martie! Great Scott, what's wrong?"

"Nothing," answered his twin, wiping away with her handkerchief the little drops of water which had gathered about her mouth and chin. "Only I couldn't see her, and I didn't know where to wait. It was so hot in the sun, and so dusty, I just kept on walking."

"Why couldn't you see her?" Sarah interrupted.

"Who did you see?" Milt wanted to know.

"Why didn't you sit on the porch and wait?" asked Pigeon.

"I don't know why I didn't," Martie answered Pigeon first. "Maybe it would have been better. I'm so hot and tired. But the person who came to the door, — I guess it was the nurse, — said that

Annette was lying down; she wasn't feeling well; and wouldn't I come another time? She didn't ask me to sit down — or — or anything."

"You poor thing; get in," Sarah said. "It's a pity you had all the trouble of dressing up for nothing."

"Yes, wasn't it?" Martie's tone was doleful. "Did you have a good time in the village?"

"Fine," said Rob. "We went to the book store and bought new tablets; then we went to the drug store and bought cones all round; we'd have bought you one if we'd known."

"Poor, old Martie Martin," her twin chanted. "All dressed up and nowhere to go, but home, sweet home."

Pigeon said, frowning: "I think it was horrid not to ask you in. You might have just spoken to her anyway."

"Was she a cross person?" Sarah wanted to know.

"No, she wasn't. Oh, dear me, let's go home and let me get into something else that doesn't matter. I think I'd like to climb up in the Elegant Tree and just sit there and cool off."

"Did you ask about Saturday?" Pigeon questioned and her sister nodded. "Yes, but I don't believe she is coming."

"Why not?"

"Just don't. She said she would see; she hoped Annette would be feeling better soon. She would give her my message and it was very kind of us to want her; still I don't believe she is coming."

Martie was right, there was a telephone message next day which explained that Annette Curtis would not be able to come to spend the day with the Martin children. She hoped to see them very soon however. She was too sick to spend the day away from home.

It was Mrs. Martin who next went to see little Annette Curtis.

Yes, she saw her, she reported to the interested little Martins that evening; she was a sweet-looking child, rather quiet and not very strong, she imagined. She was lying on a couch in the library reading a book when Mrs. Martin had gone in. She had been sick, she said, but was somewhat better now. She was sorry not to have seen Martie, and sorry not to have been able to come to spend the day at the Martin House.

" Did you ask her again to come, Mother? " the children asked.

" I did," was the reply. " I asked her to come and have tea with us tomorrow afternoon. I told her I would send for her with the car about four."

" What did she say? "

" That she would like very much to come, my dears."

" We'll see her then."

When the children came from school next day there was Mother waiting for them and looking disappointed. "Annette can't come," she told them. "Her leg is giving her some trouble today and she is lying down."

"She seems to be always lying down," Sarah said. "Just think, she's been here almost a week, and we haven't seen her yet."

"Lots of good we are doing her," Milt laughed. "Maybe she'll go, and we won't even have so much as a squint at her."

"It begins to look very much that way," their mother answered. "Her grandmother asked that you see all that you could of her. I don't quite understand it. The child seemed lonely, too, the other day when I was there. If she can't come to you then why doesn't she ask you to come to her? I am rather puzzled."

"Let's all of us go to see her anyway," Sarah suggested. "Maybe she's bashful about asking us, Mother."

"She did not appear in the least bashful," answered Mrs. Martin. "Still, go by all means; maybe the child just isn't used to children and doesn't know how to proceed."

"We'll show her," they exclaimed, and set off next afternoon all five strong.

Before very long they were traveling the same road back again without having so much as laid eyes upon the mysterious little Annette Curtis. A most disgruntled lot they were to be sure.

"There's some funny business about this

thing," Milt said, as he slapped the reins upon Danny's fat side. "Get up there, slow poke! Whose funeral you think this is anyway? Something funny about this thing, if you ask me."

"I for one am not going there again, that's certain sure." Martie spoke in an injured voice.

"If she doesn't want to see us I'm sure she needn't bother to," Sarah's chin was high.

"It takes a girl to act like that," Rob's tone was scornful of girls in general. "You wouldn't catch a boy actin' like that. No, sirree, a boy'd have more sense than to act so; a boy'd want to know folks and be friendly; any fellow would."

"Sure," agreed his brother.

"And I did so want to know how many dolls she had," Pigeon sighed.

Mary Ann called to them as they drove past the kitchen on their way to the stable. "Jus' like yo' all to ride right off and forget 'em," she said. "After I'd gone to all the trouble of makin' them cookies; birds, rabbits an' the like; off yo' go and leave 'em behind."

Martie said regretfully: "Oh, Mary Ann, we did forget the cookies, but you know we didn't do it on purpose. It was just that we weren't thinking."

Mary Ann was not appeased. "The last thing I says to yo' was: 'Don't go off and forget to take along them cookies. I left 'em on the table in the hall where yo'd be sure to see 'em,' I says, but a lot of good it did tellin' yo'!"

"But I say, we didn't do it on purpose, Mary Ann; we forgot."

"Hu!"

"Why can't Jim take them along now?" Milton asked, and Mary Ann answered: "Jim's gone to the village to have something or other done to the car. All my hurryin' for nothin'!"

"We didn't see the little girl," Pigeon tried to pour oil upon the troubled waters. "So we couldn't have given them to her anyway."

"Yo' could have left 'em, couldn't yo'? Your mother wanted her to have 'em good and fresh and all that. Sure yo' could have left 'em."

"Aw, rats!" cried Milt. "I'll ride back on my wheel and take the precious cookies, if that will make you stop fussing."

"Will yo' now?" Mary Ann beamed. "I always said yo' was a nice boy for all your villainy, Milt Martin."

Riding along in the sweetness of the late afternoon Milton whistled softly as he went up a hill, down a hill, as the road dipped and curved its way under fine, old trees and out again into the sunset which was crimsoning all the world about him. Every now and then he refreshed himself with a bite from one of the handful of cookies that Mary Ann had bestowed upon him as a reward for service. As he neared the Oaks his bicycle began a series of distressful bumps so that he dismounted to see what was wrong with it. The tire needed pumping up, so he decided to go in at the driveway leading to the garage and see if he could borrow a pump there. He walked along pushing his wheel until he reached the garage and was lucky enough to find a pump inside. Then, having filled his tire with air, he set forth across the lawn towards the front entrance to deliver the box of cookies, when he caught sight of a little girl at one of the upper windows watching him. He knew at once that it was the mysterious stranger whom none of them had even been able to see.

"Why," thought Milton, "since the cookies are for her, and here she is, why go all the way around to the front door? Why not give them to her here?" Very close to the window where she sat there grew a tall hickory tree. Now trees to any one of the five little Martins were as easy to climb as a pair of stairs, and Milt proceeded to climb at once.

"Say, up there, I've something for you," he called, holding the box so that she could see. "Wait right there and I'll bring 'em up to you."

"Oh, but you'll fall!" She was leaning out of the window, breathlessly watching him as he came rapidly up the tree towards her.

"Not a chance," he laughed. "Easy as A. B. C. Do you like cookies?"

She nodded. "Ever so much; if they won't make me ill."

"Cookies never made anybody ill yet," he announced as he swung out like a monkey, to rest on the big limb directly opposite her window. "I've eaten six on the way over and I could eat a lot more if I had 'em. Here, catch!"

The box sped through the open window. She sprang aside quickly, ducking to keep from being hit. "I guess you aren't much of a catcher," Milt grinned. "You are Annette Curtis, aren't you?"

"Yes, of course."

"Then it's all right for you to have the cookies. We forgot to bring 'em with us this afternoon when we came; went right smack off and left 'em on the hall table. So I hustled back to bring 'em to you. Say, why didn't you see us when we came this afternoon?"

He settled himself, legs fastened about the limb of the tree to hold him steady, arms free, while above his uncovered head the green leaves fluttered gaily. He seemed so strong, so sure of himself, seated there; almost as if he were a part of the tree itself. The child in the window drew in her breath in wonder that anyone could be so absolutely unafraid. "Oh, suppose you should fall!" she cried out. "You — you might be killed, you know."

"Shucks! I've climbed lots higher trees than

this. I say, why didn't you let us in this afternoon? We all came to see you."

" I couldn't," she told him. " I was lying down; my head ached. It is always aching," she answered gloomily.

" That must be pretty rotten," Milton said sympathetically, and asked: " What about your leg, is it 'most well? "

" I — I guess so; I don't know," was the fretful answer. " Something is always hurting, it seems to me."

" Maybe," — he reached up to pluck one of the leaves over his head, — " it's 'cause you keep thinking about it. Maybe you stick around too much by yourself and think of things. Say, why don't you come along over to our house and play with us, instead of staying here all the time? "

" Oh, I couldn't," she answered quickly. " I'd be sure to hurt my leg or something. You see I have to take such good care of it; once it's been broken, you know, it will never be quite strong again."

" Boloney! Say, who told you all that bunk I'd like to know? Why I broke my arm last summer — right arm too — and it's just as good now as it ever was. I learned to do lots of things with my left hand while I was getting well. . . . Whoever told you all that rot about never being strong again didn't know what they were talking about."

" Oh, but I'm sure it won't. Mrs. Owens doesn't

think it will either. She's sure I'll always have to be very careful with it."

Milt told her with great assurance: "Well listen here. Mrs. Owens doesn't know what she's talking about. She never broke anything, did she? Well, I have. I've broken an arm, so I do know. You won't be able to tell which one it was that was broken, after a little. I say, my sister Martie was dreadfully cut up about not seeing you."

"Yes, I'm sorry, but you see I was resting. I'd been out for a little while in the garden that morning, so Mrs. Owens thought I'd better lie down all afternoon; my head ached too."

Milton stared at a person who was obliged to rest all the afternoon because of being out a little while in the morning. "You must be awful delicate," he said.

"Yes I am," she nodded assent. "Everything makes me sick. I'm not a bit like other children. I can't do the things they can do."

The boy said, resting comfortably upon his high seat: "I bet you could if you tried. I bet you'd like it a lot if you'd come over to the Martin House and see our pond and the Elegant Tree and all that."

"The what kind of tree?"

"The Elegant Tree. It hangs over the pond; if you'll come I'll show you. And say, wouldn't you like to see our pets? You needn't walk about;

you could ride Danny all about the place. Danny is our pony."

"But I might fall."

"Sure you might — but you won't. Why should you? If you like I'll give you a rabbit; we've lots of 'em. You could have a run made here and feed him yourself."

"Could I? I never had a rabbit. I've a dog at home, but he's so rough when he gets to playing, I was afraid he'd knock me down and hurt my leg again; so I left him at home."

Milton said: " I bet he hated being left! It was rather a shame, don't you think, with all this space for him to run about in? "

She said again: " Still he might have hurt me . . . he is rather rough at times."

"Well what of it? " was the answer. "You aren't glass or china either, for that matter. Well so long, I've got to be getting back; good-bye."

"Oh, please don't go!"

"It's getting late."

"But stay just a little longer. I haven't thanked you for the cookies. Do tell me about the rest of you; there are five, aren't there? "

Milt said, as he swung a leg idly: " If you want to know, why don't you come and see for yourself? "

"I'd like to, only I'd be sick if I did; I know I should. I'm not a bit strong."

"Suit yourself," and he began to make ready to depart.

"Now you're mad at me. Please wait; don't go yet."

"You talk such an awful lot of rot," was the scornful answer. "I never saw anybody who was always thinking about being sick like you. I say, if Martie talked like that I'd — I'd bump her a good one!"

She asked suddenly: "Would you like to bump me a good one? Would you?"

"Yes."

"Do it!" she cried eagerly. "I never had anybody say anything like that to me before. Does it hurt?"

"There you go again!" he exclaimed. "Always thinking about being hurt."

She asked: "What would Martie do if she had broken her leg — if things were always hurting?"

He said, looking her straight in the eye: "Be a good sport. Be a sport, and not whine about it."

"You don't think I'm a good sport, do you?"

"No."

"Oh!"

She drew in her breath quickly, it was almost like a sob. For the first time in all her life she wanted to be considered a good sport; her cheeks were pink with the greatness of her desire. She leaned far out of the window to question:

"What — what would Martie do if everything

made her ill? Say, what would Martie do then?"

The boy in the tree answered at once: "She'd go right ahead and try anyway; she'd take a chance, Martie would. She wouldn't just give up and let things down her."

"O — h."

Again there was that quick sigh, a sob stifled before it had time to become one. Then: "I — I'd like to see your sister Martie. Is she anything like you?"

"Rather. We're twins, you know."

"How perfectly splendid! Grandmother told me about the Martin twins; is Martie the other?"

Milton grinned. "We're it. When we were babies Father changed the ribbons one day and fooled everybody. Well, so long."

"Wait! Please wait! There's something I want to say to you."

He called over his shoulder: "Go ahead then; shoot; what is it?"

She cried with a rush of words: "Tomorrow — tomorrow I'll go to your house. I'll see the Elegant Tree and the rabbit!"

"Yes, you will — not. By tomorrow you'll have a headache, or something; you won't come."

She asked earnestly, intently, her hands clasped tightly upon the window sill: "Martie would, even if she had a headache, wouldn't she? A — a good sport would, wouldn't she?"

He had begun to slide toward the trunk of the tree, and she had to call to make him hear. Her voice sounded as if she had been running to catch up and was all out of breath; and yet she had been sitting still at the window all the time. What she said was:

"I'll go, no matter what; I'll go tomorrow; you'll see."

Midway the tree he answered: "Right-O! Martie and I'll come for you in the pony cart tomorrow after school." And he went sliding quickly out of sight.

Out of sight but not of hearing. He could hear a gentle, lifeless voice from the room above, asking: "My love, to whom were you speaking? I heard you talking to someone as I came up the stairs just then."

The little girl's voice, high, excited, eager, answered: "One of the Martin twins. See, he brought me these; a box of cookies! He climbed up the big tree yonder and tossed them in at the window."

Then the other voice; it belonged to Mrs. Owens he was certain. "Climbed the tree! My! my! suppose he had fallen, my darling! How terribly nervous it must have made you, just watching him. Why didn't he take the cookies around to the front door? Just when you are recovering from one of your bad headaches. Oh, dear me! how unfortunate!"

"But he didn't make it worse; it's better."

The anxious, worried, fretful voice went on. "I hope so. I certainly hope so; the excitement is so bad for you. Lie down, dear child, and rest now. After dinner I'll read to you. No, don't eat the cookies, they aren't good for you I'm sure; they'll make you sick."

"The Martin boy said that cookies never made anybody sick; he ate six on the way over."

"What an exceedingly greedy little boy! They are all of them such strong, healthy-looking children; not a bit like you, my love. How could they possibly know what would be bad for a tender, delicate, little girl who has to be so careful — so *very* careful always?"

"Bunk!" exclaimed the boy under the tree, who, having disregarded the fact that listeners seldom, if ever, hear any good of themselves, had quite shamelessly eavesdropped. "Sweet Papa! just suppose you had to tune in on that all day!"

Next afternoon when the wicker cart, bearing the Martin twins, rattled up to the door of The Oaks, Annette was ready and waiting for them. Rather a white, shaky Annette to be sure, with circles under her eyes, and lips from which all the color seemed to have been drained; still, waiting for all that.

"My precious child!" sighed Mrs. Owens, mentally wringing her hands. "Change your mind, sweetheart. Give it up. You've been ill all morning; you are certain to be worse. Please listen to me, darling; wait! Some other time, perhaps."

"We'll take very good care of her," Martie said politely.

It was Milton, however, who caused the violet eyes to sparkle, in spite of their shadows, and brought a flush of pleasure to the thin, little face.

"Gee, Annette!" he exclaimed, "you're a sport all right! . . . I'll tell the world you're a bully, good little sport."

CHAPTER IV

Jimmie Adkins goes A-Fishing

"MOTHER," little Rob Martin asked at breakfast one bright Saturday morning, "may I go fishing with Jimmie today?"

His mother smiled across the table at her small, trustworthy son with the nice, gray eyes and friendly smile.

She nodded: "Are you planning to take along a lunch or will you come home for it?"

"Lunch, please," Rob answered. "It takes such heaps of time coming home. Jimmie and I 'spect to do a lot of fishing today."

"Good," his mother told him. "I'll have Mary Ann put up some sandwiches, and you two boys must be careful to come home before the sun goes down, Bobby."

"Yes'm," was the answer. "We will."

His mother was satisfied, for she knew that he would keep his word. That was one satisfactory thing about little Rob Martin; he always kept his word. One could always count on his keeping it.

Jimmie Adkins and Rob were the best of friends. The Adkins grounds joined those of the

Martins, and the two small boys had been friends since childhood. Jimmie, who was a year younger than his friend, was rather a lonely child, his mother having died when he was a baby. His life had been spent in the company of servants for the most part; for his father's business kept him away from home. Mrs. Martin encouraged the little boy to come often to the Martin House; an invitation which Jimmie accepted as frequently as possible. Scarcely a day passed without the two friends seeing each other.

In the woods back of Jimmie's house there was a jolly brook, wherein the two boys fished hours upon hours, sometimes with success, sometimes without; still it was fun either way. Today as Jimmie waited for Rob to come, he cast his line into the water, and almost immediately there was a tug. Down went the cork, and he drew in a fish, a beautiful trout, glistening in the sunshine.

Usually the small boy would have been wild with excitement over such a piece of luck; but today there was no rejoicing in him. The fishing excursion to which he had looked forward so eagerly had been spoiled. Far too miserable to wait for Rob's coming, he had wandered down to the brook to sit there in a gloom so dense that even the catching of a fish so splendid could arouse no interest.

" Hey, Jimmie Adkins, why didn't you wait for me? "

Down the path came Rob, to pause in genuine admiration before his friend's catch, flapping there upon the bank. "Gol-lee, what a beauty! Gee, Jimmie, old top, what a knockout! Lady Luck was sure with you today. Say, did you have trouble landing him? Some fish that."

The smaller boy, sitting there upon the bank, never lifted his eyes from the water.

Rob, looking at him, exclaimed: "What on earth is wrong with you? Why the grouch?"

He stared at the small boy before him in surprise. Jimmie was usually such a cheerful soul. What could have happened to make him so gloomy? Yesterday afternoon the two had parted in the best of spirits, eager for their day together in the woods; and now — this.

"Sick?"

"Naw."

"Cook mad at you?"

"Naw."

"Well why don't you go on and tell a fellow what's the matter? What makes you just sit there and say nothing?"

Jimmie thrust a hand into the depths of his pocket, fished about for a moment and drew forth a crumpled envelope. "Came this mornin'," he said. "'Bout an hour ago. He didn't say nothin' 'bout it when he was home last time. Cook's mad as hops, says maybe she'll be leavin'. She says as how she'll be always pickin' on me for every little thing. She'll be always thinkin' up things to tell Dad, Cook says."

Rob interrupted; "Say, what are you talking about, Jimmie? Who'll be always telling things? Who'll be all time picking on you? Who's the letter from, anyway?"

The small boy said with a gulp: "It's from my father. He — he's gone and got married, Rob. He — he's goin' to bring her here to our house to live; they're comin' most any day now. He said he didn't send for me, 'cause he wanted us to get acquainted here. He said — he — I don't want to get acquainted! I don't want a lady comin' to our house! I don't want a step-mother! Cook says as how —"

The little fellow broke off with a sob, and Rob Martin cried out consolingly, flinging an arm about his shoulder: "Aw, Jimmie, don't you mind. Don't you go and feel all broke up about it. Maybe you'll like having a lady about, maybe you'll like it a lot. My uncle Bob got married and brought us Bettina and we like it. Maybe you'll like it too. You don't know, maybe you will, Jimmie."

Jimmie shook his head, refusing comfort: "No I won't either."

"How you know you won't till you try?"

"Well I know. I just won't. Step-mothers are dreadful mean to little boys, they are."

"What makes them?"

" I dunno, but they are. Sometimes they turn 'em right out in the rain and snow and all. Yes, siree, if they don't do exactly what they tell 'em to do, they are awful mean. Cook says she'll be forever makin' up things to tell Daddy, so he won't like me any more. She says he'll listen to anything she tells him and he won't listen to a single thing I say."

Rob scoffed, as he patted the small, shaking shoulder, " Jimmie, don't you go listening to that old cook of yours. She thinks she knows all there is to know about everything; more than anybody else. Don't you pay any attention to her."

" I might run away," Jimmie brightened somewhat at the prospect. " I might run away and join a circus. I guess my Dad would be sorry then. I guess that maybe he'd wish he'd gone and let things alone, and not brought a lady home to live at our house and be always picking on me."

" I wouldn't run away yet if I were you," Rob advised. " Say, I'd stick around and see what she was like first; and don't you be listening to that old cook either."

In spite of his friend's advice Jimmie was far too miserable to be able to put his mind upon the fishing. In spite of the luck that he had had that morning, he was restless and unable to sit still. " Say," he told Rob, " I'm goin' to see 'bout our trap; maybe we've caught somethin'; maybe there's a bear in it."

The two little boys had set a trap in the thickest part of the little wood and it was their hope that some day they might find some large animal imprisoned therein. " All right," Rob answered. " You go ahead and I'll come along after awhile. If there's anything there just you give a yell and I'll come a-running."

The smaller boy disappeared. Rob sat on, hoping to catch a fish like the one Jimmie had caught, but this was plainly not his lucky day. Fish as he would the bobbing cork remained stubbornly upon the surface of the water; so presently he gave it up and went in search of his companion. As he walked deeper into the woods he raised his voice and shouted for Jimmie, who answered not very far away.

"Find anything? " Rob asked as he came up.

" Naw; but say, Rob, I'm pretty certain somethin's been in that old trap."

" What makes you? See any signs? "

" Well not exactly," was the answer. " But say, that old trap doesn't look just like it did when we left it last time. I wouldn't be s'prised if somethin' hadn't come nosin' 'bout in the night. These big game they're pretty smart, yo' know; they're hard to catch, they are."

Rob nodded. " You bet. Just you wait, Jimmie. What you want to bet we won't catch something in that old trap yet? "

" Sure we will. S'pose we was to catch a bear,

Rob, what would yo' do? Oh, gee! s'pose we was to catch a big, old bear; what would yo' do then?"

"Run like anything, I guess."

"Aw, I wouldn't!" was the scornful answer. "I wouldn't run, no siree!"

"Yes, you wouldn't!"

"I wouldn't. I'm not scared of any old bear! Yo' know what I'd do? I'd steal right up behind him and I'd give him a big whack — bim! — with an axe or somethin'; right in the head. Then I'd drag the body home and we could stuff it and have a show."

"That's right, we could!" Rob's eyes were bright. "We could have a dandy show right in your old barn. Gee, Jimmie, couldn't we have a bully show? — Everybody'd want to come to it. We could charge a nickel."

"'Tain't no use in plannin' a show in our barn," Jimmie Adkins interrupted dismally. "We went and forgot all about her. She'll be there and she wouldn't let us; so 'tain't any use to plan, even if we did catch a bear."

"Maybe she would, Jimmie."

"Shucks, she wouldn't! She'd be scared to death of a bear, she would. Even a dead bear she'd be scared of; yes siree!"

"Aw, you don't know whether she would or not. You haven't ever seen her; how do you know she'd be scared?"

"I just know she would. I bet she's the kind

what's scared of everything — scared of bugs and
snakes, little old grass snakes even; scared of a
weenie, teenie mouse that can't do nothin' but
run. I bet she's the scary kind all right. I just bet
she wouldn't step a foot in this wood, not fer
anythin'."

"I don't see how you know so much about
her," Rob answered. "Come on, let's go along
back, these biting flies are most eating me up.
Besides I'm hungry, aren't you?"

"What good yo' s'pose bitin' flies are?" Jimmie wanted to know as they turned back towards the brook. "Say, I hope you've got a lot
of sandwiches, Rob, 'cause I haven't got a thing
'cept some old, dry biscuit. Cook was cross 'bout
Dad's letter and wouldn't fix me anything. She
wouldn't even put any jam in between; just old
dry biscuit. Cook's mean as anythin'; sometimes."

They tramped through the stillness of the
wood, fighting off the biting flies which circled
about their heads. As they neared the brook, Jimmie exclaimed, pointing: "Look, there's a fellow
gone and got our place. He's built himself a fire
and he's fryin' bacon. Smell it; don't it smell
bully? I hope he hasn't gone and bothered our
fish."

"It isn't a fellow," Rob answered. "It's a girl.
See she's got a basket; she must be going to have
a picnic all by herself."

Rob was right. It was a girl in knickers, and not a boy as Jimmie had supposed. She glanced up as the two little boys approached, and smiled a greeting. " Somebody has had wonderful luck this morning," she said, pointing to the speckled trout lying on the bank. " This is yours, isn't it? "

Rob answered: " It's Jimmie's. He's had all the luck there is today."

She nodded. " I haven't had any luck so far. I'm going to try again after lunch. I wonder," she asked, " if you boys wouldn't like to stop and have some lunch with me. Perhaps, if you will contribute the fish, we can have quite a spread. I've an apple pie in that basket and a number of other things."

Jimmie was nudging Rob from the rear. " Tell her yes," he whispered, " 'cause those old biscuit is awful poor eatin'. I like apple pie a lot, don't you, Bob? "

" Thank you, ma'am," Rob Martin said. " Jimmie and I'd like it fine. We'll fix the fish for you; it won't take a minute."

" Good! "

There was a flash of white teeth as she stooped to place another slice of bacon in the pan over the fire. She was very pleasant to look at with her curling hair cut short about her head, her cheeks pink from the fire and her dark eyes bright and interested in what she was doing. She looked as though this was by no means the first day that she had spent in the out-of-doors; for her arms and face were tanned a lovely, golden brown, and where her white blouse opened at the neck her throat was brown also. Her movements were quick and certain as though she knew what she was about; both little boys liked her at once. A girl who knew how to build a fire in the woods and who could cook things that smelled delicious wasn't to be lightly regarded by any means. Both pairs of eyes, brown and gray as well, were regarding her with respect by the time the fish was browned to a turn and ready to serve.

"You haven't told me your names," she said as she placed a piece of the trout upon a paper plate and handed it to Jimmie. "I know that Jimmie is the lucky one today, but which of you is Jimmie?"

"This is Jimmie," Rob told her. "I'm Rob Martin. Jimmie and I play together all the time; we live near each other."

Jimmie was fairly bursting to ask a question: "How'd yo' know just how to go 'bout makin' a fire?" he demanded.

She laughed. "Oh, that wasn't hard! I'm used to going on camping trips with my brother. He's taught me everything he knows about such things. I suppose you've been lots of times yourself."

Jimmie shook his head. " I haven't ever been, not once. Dad was goin' to take me, but he never has. He keeps puttin' it off."

"You must go some time," she said. "It's really great fun. Some of us spent two weeks last summer, camping out in the Maine woods. We had a beautiful time." She glanced at the small boy who was regarding her so intently. " Since this seems to be Jimmie's lucky day," she said smiling, " suppose we let him cut the pie; what do you say?"

Her words brought back the remembrance of his trouble to the little boy. He frowned as he answered quickly: " This isn't my lucky day. This is the very most unluckiest day I ever had!"

"My goodness!" she exclaimed. "I never would have believed it after seeing that fish."

"Well, 'tis, all the same," Jimmie insisted. "It's my worst luck day of any there is."

"As bad as that?"

He nodded solemnly. "Yes'm. I guess that maybe catchin' that old trout is the last nice thing that'll ever happen to me. Everythin's goin' to be a lot different from now on."

"That's too bad," she told him, her eyes full of sympathy. "I'm beginning a new life myself today; a very different one from the life I've always led, so perhaps I can feel for you, Jimmie."

Jimmie demanded staring. "Is somebody comin' to live all the time at your house?"

"Rather the other way around," she answered. "I'm leaving a big family — three brothers and two sisters besides my dear mother and father — and I'm going to make my home in a new place."

"What makes you want to leave and go somewhere else?" Rob asked.

She was silent for a moment, then she said. "I decided all of a sudden, one day last week, to be married; so I was and here I am, as Jimmie says, with all my life different. Starting all over again in a brand new place."

From the depths of his troubled heart Jimmie Adkins exclaimed fiercely: "What did yo' want to go and get married for when yo' was havin' a good time and all? I can't see what folks want to be always gettin' married for."

The tall girl gave the fire a poke with the end of her stick. "Well, you see," she said, "I happen to care a good deal for the man I married, and I want to make a home for him, and his little boy. They have both been rather lonely, I'm afraid."

Little Jimmie Adkins spoke out of vast experience: "It's dreadful bad to be lonesome. It makes yo' feel funny inside."

The eyes of the girl were tender as she spoke to the small boy beside her. "I trust the little boy I'm going to make a home for will never know what it is to be lonely again. I hope that he is going to like having me. I hope that he's going to like having Tiger."

"Who's Tiger?" exclaimed both boys at once.

She answered: "Tiger is the big, white collie I raised from a tiny pup. I wanted to bring the nicest present that I could think of to my husband's little son; and so I brought Tiger as the very nicest present I could give. Do you think the boy will like having him?"

"Gee!" cried Jimmie Adkins. "Aw, gee, what boy wouldn't!"

There was a world of longing in his voice, and in his eyes, for if there was one thing that Jimmie desired above everything else that thing was to possess a dog of his own. His father would have given him one long ago had it not been for Cook. In vain the small boy pleaded and stormed. Cook absolutely refused to have a dog about. A boy was enough to have to straighten up after, she declared, without adding a dog.

"Where's he now?" Jimmie asked.

"I left him guarding the luggage," she answered. "There didn't seem to be anyone about, except a very cross person in the kitchen; so I told Tige to stay at home and look after things until I returned. You see my husband had to go to the village to see about some business which would keep him until dinner time. I thought it much too lovely a day to spend indoors, so I packed a basket with some of the things we had bought on the way home and — here I am."

"Where's the boy? Did you see him?"

Rob asked the question although he felt certain that he knew the answer. His heart was fairly thumping with excitement; everything was turning out so splendidly. He was glad — he was very happy — for his chum. A mother like this and a big, white collie dog for his very own!

She was saying with a smile: "There wasn't a sign of the boy anywhere about the house; although I rather think that, if I'm not mistaken, I've found him now."

She turned and held out a hand to Jimmie. "We are going to be the best of friends, aren't we, Jimmie Boy? You and I and Tiger? You'll like having Tige, won't you?"

"Aw gee!" Every little freckle stood out upon Jimmie Adkins' round face, while into his eyes there came a sudden glad light. He tried to say something but could only gulp and murmur eagerly, fearfully: "Did — did Cook say I might keep him?"

With both of his little brown fists held tightly in that of this brand-new mother's the answer came carelessly, as though it were of no importance at all:

"I really didn't ask her; of course you are to keep him, dear."

"Aw, gee!" breathed little Jimmie Adkins

again. " Aw, gee! " He closed his eyes in a very ecstasy of rapture, to open them after a moment to say:

" Is this my lucky day? Is it? I'll tell the cock-eyed world it is! "

CHAPTER V

RAIN

IF their cousin Sarah hadn't been taken ill; if their mother and father hadn't had to leave home and go to her; if it hadn't rained steadily for two days and a half; things might not have happened. However, cousin Sarah had been taken ill and had sent for Mother and Father, who had gone away immediately in Father's car. The children had been left to the care of Mary Ann; and soon after it had begun to rain.

Drip! drip! drip! upon the roof of the Martin House. Would it ever stop? Apparently not. Five disconsolate faces gazed out upon a world damp and utterly cheerless, a garden soggy and drooping. The sun had become discouraged, after trying to peep through that gray wall of clouds, and had gone away to shine somewhere else.

The five little Martins wished that they too might go away somewhere else — anywhere else.

They were tired of the house, tired of themselves, tired of everything. Five restless little bodies were crying to be out and away; five bored little noses were pressed against the windowpane; five pairs of eyes gazed out upon a garden drenched with rain and yet which called to them. Five eager pairs of feet would have rushed forth, pellmell, long ago, had it not been for Mary Ann, who stood as a barrier between them and freedom. Mary Ann blocked the way, and because of that they did not feel as kindly as they might have toward Mary Ann.

"Cross old thing!" they said of her.

Somehow it helped tremendously, just the calling of Mary Ann names. One forgot for a moment that one was shut up in the house when one's mind was at work thinking up names to call Mary Ann; and indeed, among them they managed to think up a good many.

"She's a pig!"

"She's a fat old jailer, she is!"

"She's a bossy old woman! She — she's an alligator!"

"She's a bear! She's an elephant!"

Pigeon shut her eyes tightly, then she opened them to say: "She's a prig, that's what she is; a prig — a prig, old Mary Ann."

Sarah asked: "What's a prig?" She asked it of Martie.

Martie answered: "Why, don't you know?"

Sarah shook her head. "That's why I'm asking; what is it?"

Martie looked wise and intelligent and very, very superior. She smiled. "Ask Milt, he will tell you."

Milt exclaimed: "Why pick on me?" He shut his eyes as if he were busy thinking up a name; only he wasn't; not really.

"It was Pigeon who called her that one. Why don't you ask her?" he said.

Sarah turned to Pigeon. "What is a prig? I want to know."

Pigeon was busy drumming on the glass, looking far away and dreamy. Having decided not to think up any more names she had let her mind wander to other things. That bit of shrubbery for instance down near the foot of the garden; how queerly it was behaving. Now it seemed to bend down until it touched the ground; then up it would fly again.

Sarah tugged at her arm. "What is a prig, Pigeon? Tell me, I want to know."

"A prig," murmured Pigeon. "Look, it's doing it again and there isn't any wind to make it. It's dancing a jig. What makes it?"

"Well, Pigeon, why don't you go on and tell me? What is it?"

Pigeon answered without turning her head. "That's what I'm trying to find out. There, behind that bush, don't you see? There it goes again. Look!"

"But it was you who said it, Pigeon. You called her that yourself, you know you did."

Pigeon cried out. "It isn't the bush that's doing it; it's the queer thing that's making the bush quiver and bend, and — Oh, look, it's moving! it's moving! Going up and down! There, at the end of the garden; don't you see it? What *do* you s'pose it can be? "

Four little Martins cried out: "What queer thing? What's moving? Where? Show us, show us what you mean." Sarah asked excitedly: "Is it a prig? Is it a prig you see, Pigeon? "

Pigeon answered: "I don't know what it is, but it's down there almost at the end of the garden, just behind the syringa bush. Don't you see? "

They pressed their noses to the glass. Sarah whispered half to herself: "I do hope it's a prig; I never saw one."

Milton climbed upon a chair to see above the heads of the others. After a moment he exclaimed: "It's not a prig; it's a mule; an old gray mule, that's what it is."

Sarah murmured disappointedly: "O-h-h! " And Pigeon asked: "What's an old gray mule doing in our garden anyway? "

"Oh, I see him now! " Martie's blue eyes were open wide. "There he is, there behind the syringa bush. When he moves he shakes the bush, and that's what makes it dance and act queerly."

Rob said: "But he isn't moving, he is standing quite still, only his head is moving and his foot; his front foot. He takes it up and puts it back again right in the same spot; see him! Watch!"

"There isn't any rope on him," Milt cried out, almost tipping over the chair in his effort to see plainly. "He hasn't on any harness. He's just standing there doing nothing but lifting up one foot and putting it down again, silly old thing; and shaking his head up and down, up and down."

Martie said: "Maybe he's gone and hurt his foot, Milt; maybe that's why he keeps doing it. Maybe it's broken or something."

Rob told her: "Can't be broken, Martie, or he couldn't lift it up; besides how'd he get into our garden if his foot was broken, I'd like to know? Say, I wonder how he did get in?"

Pigeon, proud of having been the one to have made the discovery, exclaimed: "I guess he just jumped right over the wall and landed there. Maybe he's a circus mule; a circus mule wouldn't mind a little thing like a stone wall."

From his stand on the chair Milt replied scornfully. "Not that old moss-back there; he couldn't jump anything. He couldn't jump as high as my hand, not that old boy."

Pigeon was not convinced. "You don't know, Milt. He may be just fooling us by standing there looking so sad and everything. He may be a fiery mule after all."

Martie cried out: "Never mind what kind of a

mule he is; if he keeps on he'll dig up Mother's syringa bush, he will!"

"Silly old thing," Milton said again. "I wonder why he doesn't go away or do something?"

"He'll dig it up, he'll hurt it; I just know he will." Martie was distressed. "Mother loves that syringa; she wouldn't want it spoiled, not for anything."

"He mustn't dig it up," Rob told them. "He mustn't; we mustn't let him."

"How'll we stop him?" Sarah asked.

Rob answered: "We've just got to stop him some way."

Pigeon thought if they raised the window and shouted to him they might make him go away. Rob thought that if they did he would leave where he was and go trampling on the flower beds; which would be worse.

"I say, he's hurting the bush," Milt exclaimed. "We've got to make him quit."

He sprang down from the chair. His cheeks were red, his eyes were dancing, he was no longer bored; "I'm going right out, folks," he cried, "and drive that old mule away."

"I'll go along and help you," Rob told him. "Soon as I find my cap."

"Oh, Milt!"

Martie looked at her twin and there was longing in her glance; longing to go with him, longing to see the garden and the old gray mule, longing for adventure, weariness of keeping still. "Why can't we all go?" she asked.

"Of course," her twin nodded. "Only I'll be the one to drive the mule. Come on, let's beat it."

They made for the door with one accord; then they stood stock still, for Pigeon had breathed a word. That word was Mary Ann.

Milton flashed upon her: "Gee, why did you have to go and say that?"

"If only Mother were here, she'd let us," exclaimed Martie.

"If cousin Sarah hadn't gone and got so sick," Sarah said.

"But Mother isn't here and cousin Sarah is sick, so let's go anyway. Let's not say anything to old Mary Ann."

It was Martie who spoke.

"Let's," agreed the other four Martins. "Let's hurry right away before Mary Ann begins to wonder why we are so quiet and comes poking in here to see for herself. Let's go this very minute."

"Who minds that old Mary Ann anyway?" Milt glanced at the door. "S'pose we go out the window?"

Rob helped him push it open. "Mary Ann's nothing but an old pirate. Let's hurry up."

Sarah said with a toss of her head: "Mary Ann's just an old prig, that's what she is."

Another moment and they stood shivering in the rain. How nice everything smelled! Oh, but it was good to be out after being in so long! Good to draw in great breaths of the fresh air; nice to be alive and off on an adventure like this.

At the foot of the garden they could see the old gray mule, there behind the syringa bush, awaiting their coming. They said as they glanced back at the library window:

" We had to save Mother's syringa."

How squashy the ground felt under foot; rather like walking on a beach when the tide was low. How damp Martie's curls were already, how they crinkled about her face in little ringlets!

" Isn't it fun to be out? Fun to walk through puddles and splash the water!" They wanted to shout aloud, to whistle and sing, but thoughts of Mary Ann kept them from doing so. They went forward, Milt a trifle in advance, straight down the garden over the wet grass covered with drops of water, which only needed the sunshine to make them sparkle like real diamonds.

" You'd better wait a moment, Milt; he might — there's no telling — he might do something!"

They were quite close now and staring at the old gray mule. How on earth did he happen to be there in their garden? There he stood seemingly not noticing their approach. All about him the rain fell in soft, round drops. It fell upon his thin body and made it shine; on his dejected, nodding gray head. If he minded it he showed no sign; he just continued to stand there. The syringa bush fluttered a few leaves which clung to his glistening, gray coat; one fell over his eye and gave him the appearance of having on a hat. The children laughed.

" Don't laugh! " chided Martie. " See how cold and shivery he is, poor old fellow."

" Poor old mule," agreed Pigeon. " It's horrid to be all wet."

She was beginning to realize that they hadn't stopped for wraps, not even for hats.

" Mules and horses don't mind; they're used to it," Milt told them.

" Sure," his brother agreed. " They're as used to it as anything."

The three girls were not so certain. The picture of the disconsolate animal before them was not convincing by any means. If the gray mule didn't mind he had a poor way of showing it. He was the very picture of misery as he stood there.

" I guess he's gone and got himself lost." Sarah threw back her head so that the rain might beat into her face and opened her mouth wide that the drops might fall in. " I guess maybe he just thinks he's home."

" I guess maybe he thinks he's in a nice dry stable with plenty of hay." Milt was scornful indeed. " I guess maybe he thinks he's an airplane stopping to rest."

"If he's lost," Pigeon asked, "why doesn't he try to get found? Why does he just stand there and do nothing about it?"

Nobody knew.

Martie the timid wondered if he was a kicking mule. "Do be careful how you go up to him, Milt."

Her brother answered: "Who's afraid?"

"You'll need a rope," Rob told him.

There wasn't any. A search through both boys' pockets brought forth only small pieces of string among countless other things, but nothing strong enough to provide a halter.

"I'll have to catch hold of his mane," Milt said.

He stepped quickly forward and placed a hand on the bent head. "Whoa!" he said, "Whoa!" and added in a loud voice and with authority: "No capers now, sir, no capers!"

The mule continued to lift his foot (it was his left foot), and to put it down again, never once looking up from the ground.

Milton patted his neck and spoke distinctly: "No kicking . . . no biting, do you hear? No capers, sir."

How brave Milt was! The four little Martins gazed at him in open admiration. How wonderful to be like Milt, never afraid of anything. Look how quiet the old mule was under Milt's masterful ways; he knew better than to try anything.

Had not Milt said, "No capers now!" And there weren't any, not a single one.

Quietly the mule stood under the firm little hand, while ever and anon he lifted up his foot and put it down again.

"Stop it!" Martie had forgotten to be afraid. "Stop it, you silly old thing; you're wetting Milt all over." But the gray mule did not stop, he went on just the same, lifting up his foot and putting it down again.

"I always knew they had no sense," Sarah declared. "They're just stupid creatures, they are. Look at him, forever doing the same thing."

Milton came to the defense of the old gray mule. "You don't know what you're talking about," he said. "Mules are as intelligent as can be. They know an awful lot, mules do. People don't begin to know just what a lot they do know, 'cause they don't go round showing off all the time, like some people."

"That's right," Rob agreed. "Mules never let on what they're thinking about . . . I bet you couldn't look at this one and guess what he's thinking; but he's thinking all right, you can just bet he is; he's thinking a whole lot. That old gray mule is doing a lot of thinking, Sarah, and don't you forget it."

"'Course he is," Milt told them. "Say, if it hadn't been for mules pulling the supply wagons out of the mud in the World War there's no telling what would have happened. They had to have supplies, didn't they? Well then, if it hadn't been for the mules to pull 'em out of the mud where would they have been, I'd like to know? I guess those old mules you think haven't got any sense helped win the war for us, I guess they did all right. Wouldn't you say that a mule who had intelligence enough to win a war, a war like that one, had sense; wouldn't you? You'd better be awful thankful the Lord went and gave us mules 'stead of saying things about them."

"Oh, Milt!" interrupted Martie, "You're being all splashed with mud yourself; look at your trousers. What a sight!"

"Well," shouted her twin, "who can go and think about trousers and capture a runaway mule at the same time I'd like to know? Say, I'm going to turn him round, so you kids look out; there's no telling what he might go and do."

The four little Martins scattered to right and left, where from a safe distance they watched Milton turn the old gray mule around and start him toward the gates which were standing wide open. They came trooping after, laughing, and talking all at once.

"Luck! The gates are open . . . that's how he got in."

"Make him run, Milt!"

"What you going to do with him?"

"Where you going to take him?"

"Want to see me climb on his back? Get up, old mule!"

"Yes, get up, old mule, get up, why don't you?"

"What you going to do with him now, Milt?"

From over his shoulder Milt answered: "I don't know. Maybe there'll be someone down in the road looking for him."

They did not find anyone down in the road when they reached the gates; there was no one out searching for the old gray mule. But they found something else. They found light and color and adventure waiting just across the road in their own meadow.

Under one of the tall hickories there stood a large wagon and a smaller one beside it. A short way off a fire burned brightly, cheerily, sending up a dancing, curling blue flame and with it a shower of sparks now and then.

Seated about the fire were people . . . people who seemed to have no thought for the drenched ground, nor for the rain which came through the thick branches and fell dripping upon them. They were laughing; and from the pot over the fire there came, on the breeze, a whiff of something cooking.

On a soiled, yet gay, blanket a plump brown baby rolled contentedly about, his black eyes very wide open, his chubby fist beating the air happily. Near by two older children played noisily with

some colored beads, while an old woman leaned
from the larger of the wagons to ask a question.

"Gypsies!" exclaimed the five little Martins.
"Gypsies! Oh, my hat!"

CHAPTER VI

Gypsies

O H! see the cunning baby! Isn't he just too sweet for anything!" Martie was pointing.

" Look at that old woman," Sarah said. " She must be his great grandmother. How dreadfully old she looks! See the tall girl stirring the pot; she's pretty, isn't she? "

" That big fellow there by the fire must be the chief," Rob said. " And it's their mule that came into our garden. Yes, sir, that old gray mule belongs to the gypsies."

" Yes," his brother agreed. " And I'm going to take him to them."

" Oh, Milt, are you? "

" Sure," said Milt, with a little swagger. " Sure I am. He's theirs, isn't he? He belongs to them, doesn't he? Well then, I'm going to take him to them."

Was anyone ever so wonderful as their brother Milt!

They watched breathless as he led the old gray mule across the road down into the meadow beyond; then they turned their attention once more to the gypsies. They were dipping whatever it was out of the pot; they seemed merry about it and there was a good deal of laughter. The two children had thrown aside the colored beads and had managed to squirm close to the steaming pot. The tall girl with the black hair threatened them with the long-handled spoon she held, and they ducked and ran away, only to return in a moment, to dodge under the big man's elbow and come close to the food the girl was dishing out to them.

The jolly brown baby began to cry; perhaps he too was hungry. A tall woman came forward, stooped and picked him up, and he stopped crying at once. She held him out to the very old woman in the wagon and he cried again. The men were eating, sitting down upon the ground, while the women hovered in the background, eating too. One of them had a red shawl thrown over her head. The fire was roaring merrily now, sending out a crimson glow which lighted the meadow in all directions.

Into the light of the fire they saw their brother Milton step, leading the old gray mule.

They saw the gypsies look up in surprise at the slender lad who stood there before them so unafraid. The fire-light turned his hair to bright gold that glistened. He held himself erect, a shining young knight among all those dusky folk; his eyes sparkled with the light of adventure. They could not hear what he said to them, nor their answer; but they saw the big man nod his head several times; they saw him point to the boiling pot and they knew that Milt was being invited to sup with them. Could anything be more thrilling? Lucky Milt! Oh, lucky Milt, indeed!

They watched Milt smile and shake his head and they knew that he was not going to sit down and eat with them, after all. He was pointing back their way and they knew that he was explaining about finding the mule in their garden. Milt was not in the least afraid, but then Milt was never afraid of anything. Now he was turning away and the big man, who must be the chief, had risen and was walking beside him. As they passed the wagon the old woman leaned far out so as to touch with one crooked old finger his shining hair. The pretty girl near the pot looked after him as if she was sorry that he was going; as if she would have liked him to stay and eat of the food she had cooked.

At the end of the meadow the big gypsy stopped and shook hands with Milton, then turned and left him, and he came on alone. Now he was running swiftly up the long sloping hillside and soon he was beside them, waiting at the stone wall and eager for his coming. They crowded about him, plying him with questions, one after another, so curious were they.

"Milt, oh Milt, the big man who walked with you, was he the chief? Do you think he was?"

"What did he say, Milt? Was the old mule his?"

"Did he thank you for bringing him back?"

"What was in the pot? Did they ask you to have some?"

"Oh Milt, did you see the darling baby?"

"The pretty girl stirring the pot, did you see her?"

"And the old woman; the old woman tried to touch you when you passed, did you know it?"

His eyes were sparkling and he was breathing fast, not entirely from his run.

"I think he was the chief; he asked me to eat with them. Sure it was their mule; his name is Bill — 'Old Bill' they called him. And say, he's blind in one eye. Yes, he thanked me for bringing him back. He asked where I lived. I don't know what was in the pot, but it smelled good. Yes, I —"

"Chil-dren! Child-ren! Martie! Milton! Sa-rah! Pigeon! Rob! come back here, this very minute; do you hear?"

It was fate in the shape of Mary Ann bearing down upon them to drag them to the house. Mary Ann, the very set of whose cap proclaimed wrath, as she hastened down the path toward them.

"Out bareheaded, without coats or anything! What do you mean? And I thought yo' was safe and sound in the library! If I take my eyes off yo' for one little minute even — I never saw such children! Yo' wait till I tell your mother. We'll see what yo' father has to say about such goings on. March yo'selves back to the house, do yo' hear?"

Martie tried to explain, but it was no use.

"There was a reason, Mary Ann." She got no farther, for Mary Ann interrupted: "I don't want to listen to no reason, Martie Martin, an' yo' drippin' wet this minute. There wasn't no reason — don't yo' be tellin' me there was — to send yo' children out in the rain like that. It's just plain badness, that's what it was!"

"But there was a reason," Pigeon tried raising her voice above that of the angry Mary Ann. "It was a mule — an old gray mule; — he was in our garden. He was digging up the syringa bush. He — ."

"Now don't be tellin' me none of yo' fairy tales, Mary Frances, this ain't the time to be talkin' 'bout fairies an' such like, an' yo' soppin' wet."

"But it wasn't a fairy, Mary Ann," insisted Pigeon. "It was a mule, I tell you, an old gray mule in our garden."

Mary Ann just wouldn't listen. Instead she hustled them protestingly up the walk, scolding at every step, and into the house. Such children! Surely they were the very worst in the world. There never were such children, five such perfect-ly outrageous children anywhere. She didn't stop talking even when they were once inside, but rushed them up the stairs and, in spite of loud objections, into hot baths and from there into their beds.

" But it's hours and hours before our bed time."

" I don't care if it is. I've got yo' now where I can keep my eye on yo', I have. In bed yo' go; in bed yo' stay!"

There was Julia, the down stairs maid, with glasses of hot milk on a tray, and Mary Ann, all red in the face and very angry, standing by to see that they drank it, not merely pretended to.

" I hate it, horrid old stuff, and I'm not sick," Sarah protested, sitting up in bed and looking very like a jolly little boy in her pink and white pajamas, like striped candy.

" Well if yo' ain't sick now, yo'll be sick to-morrow. Yo'll all be sick, see if yo're not," prophesied Mary Ann. " Did anyone ever see such children? Drink that milk, every drop, now."

Under Julia's sympathetic gaze they drank.

" Say, can we get up now? "

" Indeed an' yo' can't. In bed yo' are, in bed yo' stay, every man Jack of yo', till mornin'; and by mornin' yo' won't want to get up, I'm thinkin'."

" Mary Ann, I tell you, we aren't sick! "

" Huh! It's sick — dreadful sick — yo're goin' to be! "

"Shucks! Rain never hurts us."

"We'll see about that; anyway yo're in bed, and in bed yo' stay."

"Aw, Mary Ann, have a heart."

"None of yo' coaxin' ways now, Milt Martin. I tell yo' I won't be got 'round, no, sir! In bed yo' stay."

"Say, how about lessons?"

"Yo' can learn 'em in bed; besides yo're more than likely to stay home all day tomorrow, sick in bed."

"We'll fool you yet, you wait."

"Don't we have any supper?"

"Julia'll bring trays."

Rob called: "What's for supper? Anything good?"

Mary Ann was indignant. "Good! Anything good! Yo've got the face to be askin' me that after the way yo've behaved this day. It ought to be bread an' water, that's what it ought to be. Huh!"

Martie said sweetly from her pillow: "But it won't be, I know." She closed her eyes to think the better. "It will be something per-fect-ly lovely, I just know; maybe some of those little cakes that Mary Ann makes so beau-ti-ful-ly and — and a baked custard — perhaps other things nice."

"Maybe a gingerbread boy, with currants for eyes," suggested her twin.

"And perhaps it won't be." Mary Ann was scornful in the extreme.

Milt leaned upon one elbow, his curly hair rumpled and shining. "Now wouldn't it be ex-act-ly like Mary Ann to go and make us, say a cherry pie, one with a lot of goo in it?"

"A cherry pie indeed!" Mary Ann cast upon him a withering glance. "It takes yo' to go thinkin' up somethin' like that, Milt Martin, it does for a fact. Bad little boys, and bad little girls who run out in the rain!"

Pigeon clasped her hands over her head. "We aren't always bad," she began.

"Bad little girls and bad little boys," went on Mary Ann, unheeding. "Who don't even have the grace to say they're sorry."

Sorry! Five pair of eyes fell guiltily at the thought. They were not in the least sorry. They were glad, very, very glad; it had been delightful. They only wished that they might live to do it all over again. Gypsies, an old gray mule, the garden in the rain. Sorry! Not one of them. They couldn't be; it was asking too much to expect them to be.

"Milt," exclaimed Martie, when Mary Ann had departed disgusted, kitchenwards, "oh, Milt, wouldn't it be fun to be a gypsy? To live in a wagon and to cook things in a big pot under the trees?"

"When I'm a man," answered her twin, after a

moment's reflection, " I may take up gypsying for a trade."

" Milt, how perfectly splendid! " Martie flung aside the cover and sat up straight. " Will you take me with you? Say, will you have a wagon? And I think I'd like a little brown baby to take along, if you don't mind."

" Will you have an old gray mule to pull the wagon? " asked Pigeon.

Her brother shook his head. " Not me. I'm going to run mine by motor. I expect to travel fast, I do; no old mule for mine, no sir — ee! "

Sarah said thoughtfully: " Poor old mule! Did you say his name was Bill? I guess he wishes we had let him stay in our garden where he'd have nothin' to do but rest, 'stead of havin' to haul a heavy wagon."

" Maybe he ran away," suggested Rob. " Maybe it was because he was runnin' away that he went and hid behind Mother's syringa bush. Maybe he thought nobody would find him."

Martie ran to the window. " I thought maybe I could see the gypsies' fire, but I can't. I wonder what they are doing now? I wonder if they are dancing? Oh, do you suppose they are? Wouldn't you love to see 'em dance? I would. I'd adore to see 'em. I wish we could have our fortunes told; wouldn't it be splendid if we could? I wish to-morrow would come! "

Julia appeared with a tray.

Martie bounded back to bed and everybody sat up to see if Mary Ann had relented and sent up something nice.

There was no cherry pie, but there was toast and hot muffins and apple sauce with a little frosted cake for each one. Mary Ann was beginning to relent; by tomorrow they might expect something even better. Mary Ann was like that; her bark was far more terrible than her bite had ever been.

"Old Mary Ann's not so bad after all," Sarah said, as she helped herself to a muffin.

"There were horses tied under the tree over there, I saw 'em. Bill didn't have to pull all by himself." Rob's thoughts were not upon supper just then. "Poor old Bill! I guess he did run away sure 'nough."

Asleep at last to dream of fire light, of a meadow crimson and alluring, of a black-eyed baby upon a gay blanket; laughter; a tall man and a gypsy girl leaning over a pot; an old gray mule standing still in the rain. Then the sunshine flooding the world, dancing in at their window, flickering on the wall, calling to them — and the five little Martins were awake again.

CHAPTER VII

BILL

SUCH a day!
Breaths of cool, clear air; blue skies, dazzling sunshine. The grass all amethyst and diamonds this morning; the shrubbery glistening green and jeweled also; the world at its best after the rain.

Such a day!

Milt at the window in a blue and red bath robe drank in great draughts of the fragrant air.

" Say, folks, what would you give to be a gypsy and out on the road today? "

" Gee, wouldn't it be fine! "

"Great! "

Rob struggling with a shoe string called out: " I'll tell the world it would! "

Later, Mary Ann in the breakfast room doorway gazed with amazed eyes upon five little Martins, rosy and not a bit the worse for their adventure, putting away cakes.

" If you ain't the beatenest children! "

" Hi, Mary Ann, more cakes please! "

" And yo' don't feel sick, none of yo' ? "

" Sick, on a day like this? I should say not."

"No colds? Nobody's throat scratchy, huh?"

"Not a sniffle, not a scratch, not a bit of it."

"Then I give up!" She went back to stirring buckwheat, plainly puzzled. She had been so sure.

There was time before school to run down the road for another glimpse of the gypsies, if they hurried.

No curling fire this time, no fat baby rolling on its blanket, no boiling pot with dusky folk grouped about it, no tall dark-eyed girl, no big man, no old dame leaning from the wagon, no horses under the tree. They were gone; the gypsies were gone!

Before them the meadow lay deserted; only trampled grass and bits of charred wood marked the place where the gypsies had been. They had gone away in the night while the children slept, or else early in the morning. Gone to follow the road, gone to seek another camping ground, gone to build their fire and cook their food somewhere else. Disappointed, the children stood and gazed upon the place where they had been.

"Oh!" cried Pigeon. "I wish they hadn't gone away. I wish they'd come back in our meadow, I do. Oh, dear!"

"Me too, Pigeon," Sarah said. "I did want to see the baby again."

The others said nothing; they had counted so on the gypsies being there still. Silently they went back to the house, this time across the garden, and as they neared the syringa bush they stood still, staring.

There in the same spot stood the old gray mule, lifting up his foot only to put it down again. It was just as if he had never moved from the day before; and except that he was no longer wet, he appeared just as disconsolate as he had been yesterday and just as forlorn.

"Oh! oh!" little Mary Frances clasped both hands in rapture. "The gypsies left him for us! The dear, kind gypsies left him for us. They gave us Bill for our very own; wasn't it nice of them?"

A gift to them from their friends the gypsies.

They wanted to think so. Disappointment changed instantly to gratitude, a gratitude mingled with pride that they should have been so honored. Radiant and forgetting caution in their joy, they literally flung themselves upon the old gray mule with cries of rapture. They caressed the bony old neck and patted the bowed head. Was he not a gypsy mule? Had his days not been spent in the company of gypsies? Had he not been a part of their gay, carefree existence? Here was no ordinary mule; here was a gypsy mule, a mule who had lived and moved and had his being with gypsies.

It was a triumphant procession which marched kitchenward leading the slow-going Bill. They must show him to Mary Ann.

"Mary Ann! Mary Ann! Come and see what we have! Isn't he too splendid? The gypsies gave him to us! The gypsies did!"

They turned a deaf and indignant ear to Mary Ann's demand that they go straight off and turn that old mule out.

"Turn him out nothing! We're going to keep him for our own, we are. We're going to wash him good and clean and enter him in the pet show for next Saturday," they answered scornfully.

Their eyes were shining, their faces were radiant with delight.

"Yo' ain't ever! that bony old mule!"

"Now don't you go callin' him names, Mary Ann. Bill isn't just an old everyday mule, we'll have you know. Bill's a gypsy mule, that's what he is; a real gypsy mule."

Mary Ann tossed her head. "He's a no 'count one, as ever I've seen."

"Mary Ann!"

"If yo're asking me, he ain't worth the powder and shot it would take to shoot him; and there yo' go, talkin' 'bout puttin' him in a show. Who ever heard the like?"

"You bet we are. He'll be the only gypsy mule in the show, we can tell you that."

"He'll be the poorest, most no 'count one in the show. I can tell you that."

Their ardor in no wise dampened by Mary Ann's lack of enthusiasm, they led the tottering

Bill to an empty stall in the stable, occupied now only by Dandy, the children's pony. They filled the feed box to overflowing. Such a meal! That old mule must have imagined that he had died and gone to a heaven for mules, gypsy mules in particular, who had never known what it was not to be hungry.

It was after dusk when the children's parents arrived.

Before they could take off their wraps they were led by five excited little Martins, all talking at once, out to the stable, to view by flash light their brand-new possession.

"You know he isn't an ordinary mule, Father," Milt was explaining. "No indeed, he isn't! He's a gypsy mule, Bill is; a real gypsy mule."

"And, Mother! Oh, Mother! the gypsies left him in our garden for us." Pigeon was dancing first on one foot, then the other. "Wasn't it nice of them to go and give us such a love-ly present?"

"We're going to enter him in the pet show next Saturday," Martie told them with pride, as the rays of the flash light fell upon Bill standing dejectedly just where he had been left.

Father and Mother took one long look first at the old gray mule, then at each other. Father turned to Martie: "You are? And how do Dandy and Major take to that? Isn't it going back on old friends a bit to leave them out?"

"But you see, Father," they explained, "Bill's a gypsy mule. There won't be another pet in the show just like Bill."

"No," said their father. "No, I can well believe that."

Mother laid a hand upon his sleeve as they turned to leave the stable. "Do you think we should let them?" she asked in a whisper.

"Does it matter really?" Father smiled.

"No, I suppose not; and still Major and little Dandy are such charming pets and this—"

"My dear, this is not an ordinary mule, you mustn't forget that. He's a gypsy mule, he is." Father's eyes were twinkling.

They entered Bill on Wednesday of that week, and the rest of it was spent in getting him ready.

It was no light task; for the gypsy mule required a great deal of getting ready. With pails of water and a brush they set about it, taking turns in scrubbing Bill until their arms and shoulders ached. Still, in spite of all their labors, the gypsy mule showed no great improvement in his appearance. Martie worked hard to finish a wreath which was to encircle his neck; it was fashioned of pink crepe paper made into roses which had constantly to be renewed as Bill steadily refused to lift his head for more than the briefest moment, and the wreath kept slipping off.

Saturday morning their mother asked at breakfast:

"You still intend to enter the gypsy mule?"

"Yes, indeed, Mother. We have him most ready. Martie màde a beau-ti-ful wreath of pink roses to go round his neck. He looks perfect-ly splendid. We'll bring him round front to show you when we're ready."

Mother put down her coffee cup, and glanced uncertainly at the five happy little Martins before her. "There will be a great many very lovely pets there," she told them. "Everybody may not understand that Bill is a gypsy mule, you know."

"Oh, but they will, Mother," they exclaimed. "'Cause you see we've made a sign out of cardboard and we're going to hang it on him so everybody can see it. It says: 'This is Gypsy Bill.'"

Father put down his cup hastily. "Well, good luck," he said.

In reckoning for the pet show, however, the five little Martins had reckoned without taking Bill into their confidence; and so, at the eleventh hour as it were, they were wholly unprepared to have the gypsy mule take things into his own hands and refuse absolutely to take part in the show at all. Bill the docile, Bill the placid, had become Bill the obstinate, and he refused to budge one inch from his stall.

In vain five surprised, indignant little Martins coaxed, urged, threatened; yes, even jerked at his head and pushed at him from the rear, in their combined efforts to lead him forth. It was of no use; Bill had decided not to be led, and led he would not be.

Having tasted of luxury, Bill had no idea of returning to the road, not even for the briefest of stays. The road to Bill meant work, the stable idleness; Bill chose the stable. He knew a good thing when he saw it. Here in his stall was always plenty and to spare, there on the road there was little if anything; so why venture upon the road. The gypsy mule had had enough of the road for all time. He decided to stay where he was, and stay he did.

"Look at him," sobbed Pigeon, red in the face and entirely out of breath from pushing. "He's just the most ungratefullest mule I ever saw! He doesn't even care 'bout the per-fect-ly sweet wreath Martie went and made for him. He doesn't appreciate anything!"

"Oh, please! please! Bill darling!" coaxed Martie, holding out the wreath of pink roses. "If only you knew how nice you looked in it."

"Gypsy mule or no gypsy mule, he's just plain mean, he is!" and Sarah gave a disgusted slap to emphasize her words.

Milt, hot and dusty with a streak of mud across his face, directed them: "Listen, now, when I say, 'Ready,' I'll pull and you folks push as hard as you can. One! two! three! all together! Push! everybody;—push! Ready! Push! Shove! Did you ever see such a mule? Come on, let's try again."

"One! two! three! Ready! Shove! everybody, Shove!"

They did, but with no visible results. Bill remained as before. Not an inch had he moved.

"We'll be late if we don't start pretty soon," panted Rob. "I saw a lot of fellows goin' by with their pets."

"Well come on, let's try again," Milt said. "Maybe he'll go this time."

They tried, they tried until, thoroughly exhausted, they could try no more. Still the gypsy mule remained as stationary as ever.

Martie dropped her wreath.

"It's no use," she sighed. "He doesn't seem to care at all about it."

"I can't push any more." Pigeon wiped a hot little face with her sleeve. "I'm most dead now from tryin'. Oh, dear!"

"And it's 'most time for the show to begin," wailed Sarah. "What are we goin' to do 'bout it, Milt?"

Then, as though in answer to her question, who should appear in the door to the stable but little Dandy. "Why," he seemed to be asking, "do you bother about an old gray mule when you have me?"

The five little Martins brightened suddenly; the world seemed a less gloomy place than it had a moment ago; "Let's take Dandy instead," Rob said. "If we hurry there'll be time enough."

When they trotted up the driveway that afternoon a blue ribbon floated proudly from the pony's bridle, while Martie held in her hands a silver cup. Their pony had won first prize, and yet the disappointment of the morning was fresh with them. They had counted so on taking the gypsy mule.

"It wasn't nice of Bill when he knew just how much we wanted him to go," declared Pigeon. "It wasn't kind."

Sarah answered: "Maybe gypsy mules aren't kind. Maybe he just can't help being that way."

Milton shook his head. "There isn't a bit of use in makin' excuses for him," he told them sternly. "Bill was plumb mean, that's what he was."

Martie nodded: "And ungrateful too. He didn't seem to appreciate that beau-ti-ful wreath, after I'd gone to all the trouble of making it for him, or the sign, or — or anything! I hope he's ashamed of himself for acting so."

If the gypsy mule was ashamed, as Martie had hoped, he showed not the faintest signs of it, nor of repentance either, for that matter. He stood as they had left him, calm and unconcerned, nor did he vouchsafe so much as to cast an eye in the direction of the returning children, whose trust in him he had so badly betrayed.

"Ashamed, my hat!" exclaimed Milton in disgust. "Just look at him. Does he look ashamed, or sorry, or anything?"

He did not.

CHAPTER VIII

The Good Little Sport

MRS. CURTIS put out a hand to take up the letter lying upon her breakfast tray. A tender little smile came to play about her lips as she recognized the round, childish handwriting of her granddaughter; then the smile changed into a sigh.

Poor little Annette! She must be ill again. The letter looked as if it had been written while in bed, so many smudges adorned its one page. The dear child, she did have so many ups and downs — mostly downs.

"Dearest Grandmother," the letter read. "I want you to do something for me right away, please, Grandmother. Just as soon as you read this won't you order the car and have Alfred take you shopping? Here's a list of the things I want. First some play suits (dresses keep gettin' in the way when I climb trees or paddle about in the boat) "; the smile returned to Mrs. Curtis's lips and even crept up into her eyes; " and, Grandmother, please send me Toby. I want to have him here with me; besides I think he'd like awfully well, knowing Major and Sallie. I go over to the Martin House every day except when they come over here. Oh, yes, please, Grandmother, I'd like a fishing rod, one of the kind with a cunning, little red cork that goes bobbing up and down in the water. Jimmie and Rob are going to take me fishing next Saturday if it doesn't rain. Heaps of love and kisses. Please excuse the blots, I'm in such a tearing hurry; Martie is waiting for me.

Your loving little granddaughter,

Annette."

Mrs. Curtis put down the letter with a laugh and took up her coffee cup. Later she took it up again to go over the list of things written at the bottom of the page. After she had read them all she put out a hand and touched the bell by her side.

"Mary," she said, when the maid appeared, "please tell Alfred to have the car at the door by," — she glanced at the list once more — "by ten. I have quite a good deal of shopping to do this morning."

Down by the garage at The Oaks that morning Annette Curtis was on her knees peering into a square box with strips of wood nailed firmly across the top. Between two of the strips there appeared a pink ear, and, at times, a pink nose which twitched eagerly.

"You darling, lovely thing, you," Annette was

saying, as she slipped in a hand to caress the white fur of the rabbit who, accustomed to being petted, merely lifted pink, unafraid eyes to gaze at her. "I'm going to adore having you for my very own!"

Bunny lifted his nose inquiringly as though to say, "I don't fancy these narrow confines very much, my dear."

"Milt's coming over right after school to help me build a rabbit pen," she said as if in answer. "Just the moment it's ready I'll let you out, beautifulest; so please try and be patient, won't you? And here's another lettuce leaf."

There was the patter of small hoofs approaching at a rapid rate, the jingle of harness and the rattle of a much-used pony cart upon the driveway. Looking up, Annette saw Dandy, beautifully groomed until every bit of him shone like satin, come trotting gaily under James' guiding hand to stop with a flourish under the porte-cochère at the side.

Leaving the rabbit she hastened to where James stood beside the pony's head, waiting her coming, cap in hand.

"Mrs. Martin's compliments, Miss Annette; she thought you might have errands in the village this morning, and might be finding Dandy of use. If you say so, I'm to leave him here and some of the family will come for him when school is over."

Leave Dandy! Leave him for her to drive —

to drive to the village! Oh, she couldn't! suppose, just suppose —

"You're a good little sport, Annette," the words came back to her, — Milton's words.

She took a step forward, her shoulders straightened, and the color came flooding into her face as she tried to answer quietly, calmly, just as if driving the pony was an everyday affair; as if she were not frightened half out of her wits at the very thought.

"Thank you, James," she said, while her eyes fastened themselves on Dandy's left ear, which twitched suddenly as though he were intent on what she had to say. "Please tell Mrs. Martin I'm so much obliged to her. Yes, I have a great many errands in the village today, and I shall be glad to have Dandy."

"Very good, Miss." James swung upon his heels, touched his cap, and prepared to take his departure. "He'll stand until you are ready for him."

Until she was ready for him! Good heavens! would she ever be ready for him? Perhaps, if she wasn't feeling well — oh, but she was feeling well, it was no use to pretend that she wasn't. She hadn't had a headache in days now. Oh, my! Oh, my! what was she going to do about driving that pony?

"A good little sport."

Milton's eyes had been full of admiration as

he had said it. A good little sport — and here she was, afraid. Oh, how terribly afraid she was to drive the same pony that little Mary Frances Martin rode without saddle or bridle! Dandy, the Martin children's beloved Dandy, the very thought of him had set her heart to pounding. What was she going to do about it? Should she let the pony continue to stand where he was until Milt came later to help her with the rabbit pen? What excuse could she make to him? In her pocket at this very moment was the carefully written list of the things they would need, things like nails for instance; what should she say to Milt when he asked why she had not gone, when the opportunity to go was standing there before her?

The five little Martins thought no more of climbing into that wicker cart behind the spirited little pony than they did of going to bed at night. Away they would go — lickity split — down the road to wherever they were bound. What would they think of her when they knew? What would the twins think of her? Afraid! Afraid to drive Dandy! Why, oh, why had Mrs. Martin ever thought of sending him! Oh, dear! Oh, dear! and she did so want Milt to keep on thinking of her as a good little sport. If he knew he would never call her that again, never.

Mrs. Owens came out on the side porch and Annette braced herself; took a long breath, gathering together every scrap of her courage, clasping her hands tightly at her side, and said nonchalantly:

"I'm going to the village to do some shopping; want to come along?"

Mrs. Owens hesitated for a moment then, perhaps remembering sundry errands of her own which she would like to attend to in the village, asked: "Which one of the Martin children is driving this morning, my dear?"

"None of them," Annette answered quickly. "Mrs. Martin has sent Dandy for me to use; I'm driving."

"You!" exclaimed Mrs. Owens in surprise. "But, my dear child —"

"Yes," said Annette quietly. "I'm driving the pony myself this morning."

Mrs. Owens was staring at her as though she couldn't believe that she had heard aright. "Do you think you'd better risk it, dear? Suppose something should go wrong — he seems to be a most mettlesome little animal. Suppose — Annette, darling, do you think you had better try?"

Annette answered gently, "If you are afraid, please don't go."

In Mrs. Owens' mind duty came first, and it was plainly her duty to go if Annette was bent on so doing. So the good lady closed her eyes as she said in a voice that quavered somewhat: "Why of course I will go with you, dear child."

She went to fetch her hat and purse. When she returned Annette had taken her seat in the pony cart and was waiting for her.

"Ready?" she asked, as her companion settled herself somewhat nervously beside her. "Then let's go." She gathered the lines firmly in her hands. "Get up, Dandy," she said.

Dandy, who considered that he had stood still quite long enough, was more than willing to obey. Away he went, trotting in his best style down the drive straight through the open gates and out into the road. Once there he quickened his pace to a fast trot in spite of Annette's tug upon the reins.

"Whoa!" she cried. "Not so fast. We've plenty of time. Whoa, Dandy! please, Dandy!"

Dandy had his own opinion upon the matter. He paid not the least attention to either voice or reins; it was plain that he intended taking this trip to suit himself. Besides he was feeling particularly good that morning, so he desired to go and to go swiftly. There were certain places in the village that he enjoyed visiting. One was the fountain where he might drink, and where he was accustomed to meeting friends with whom he passed the time of day, while the young Martins did their shopping. Perhaps some of his friends were there now; they might be waiting for him. If so, he had best hurry. He hurried.

"Whoa!" exclaimed Annette, very red in the

face from her exertions upon the lines. " Whoa, I say! whoa, Dandy!"

Dandy did not whoa, nor did he even slacken his pace.

The hands upon the reins trembled. Mrs. Owens said hastily: " Why go so fast, darling? I'm sure there is plenty of time."

" I — I can't very well help it," Annette made answer. " It — it's Dandy who is in a hurry."

" Oh! " cried Mrs. Owens, clutching at her hat. " Oh, my dear, do pull him down to a walk! We are j-jolting r-rather b-badly, d-don't y-you t-think? "

Annette was of the same opinion; but Dandy was not. Dandy was, in fact, having a most elegant time. He was enjoying himself immensely; there was no doubt of that. To begin with, the touch upon the lines was so light that it was almost as if he were out for a run alone, which was exciting. Upon the road at his side there trotted the black pony he had seen before and which he well knew was his shadow (only he pretended not to). He glanced out of the corner of his eye at the black pony and shook his head defiantly. The shadow pony instantly responded by shaking his head. This, Dandy felt to be a challenge; he would out-run the shadow pony; he would leave him far behind; he would show him a thing or two.

Like a sky rocket he was off down the road,

the shadow pony racing at his side, head down, feet fairly flying.

"Annette! Oh, Annette!" screamed Mrs. Owens. "I believe, I do believe he is running away!"

Annette was sure that he was.

In vain she hung to the lines, pulling with might and main. It was not of the slightest use. Away they went, whirling down the road (fortunate for them that it was deserted at this time in the morning), the little cart swaying and bouncing most uncomfortably, terrifyingly. The little girl struggled with a wild desire to drop the reins and to bury her head in Mrs. Owens' lap. Oh, what would happen next? Would they be thrown out upon the road? What would become of them when they reached the village?

"Annette!" Mrs. Owens pitched her voice above the noise of flying hoofs and protesting wheels. "He's running away with us; what had we better do? Oh, my sakes alive, what on earth must we do?"

"Sit still; sit still and hold on tight!"

It was the good little sport who answered, who braced her feet against the dashboard and pulled back upon the lines. She wouldn't drop them, whatever happened she would hold them; she would still be holding them when the smash came. She was expecting it any moment now. Before them loomed the village, growing rapidly nearer. Already they had passed a few scattered houses on the outskirts. Wide-eyed children had run to the door to gaze at them, to send shrill cries of warning after them. Soon, very soon at this rate of speed, they would be entering the main street. What would happen as they went flying up it? What would not?

The race was almost at an end, and still the shadow pony was there. He had not been able to shake him off, try as he would; he was still there and going strong. Some runner that pony. Well, anyway, it had been fun trying.

So quickly that Mrs. Owens and Annette almost sat in each other's lap for the moment, Dandy ceased to be a runaway pony and became on the instant a gentle, well behaved, docile little animal. Quite a lamb of a pony indeed, as he settled into a jogging trot and from that to a walk, which brought him to the brown stone fountain from which he proceeded to refresh himself with great draughts of the cooling water; stepping aside to give the shadow pony some as well. But the shadow pony was gone. So, he had shaken him off after all — who said he wasn't good?

On somewhat shaky legs the two occupants of the wicker cart climbed weakly down. Were they really alive and safe? It was like a dream. All about them the quiet village street, where people went to and fro about their business. Little children played happily in the shade while their mothers stopped to gossip with other mothers in the stores and men went up and down the post-office steps quite unconcernedly. But the strangest of all was the sight of a satiny, brown pony who stood so still, so still. Had he ever moved?

Would they have the courage to step in that pony cart again?

To hide the trembling of her hands Annette slipped them hastily into her pocket; to hide the trembling of her voice she pretended to laugh as she handed the list over the counter and wondered if the list sounded as hollow to the good Mr. Jenkins, who was waiting on her, as it did to her. Mrs. Owens, after hastily adjusting her hat and powdering her nose, had gone on to the post-office and the little girl was not sorry to be left alone for a moment or two. She had made all her purchases when Mrs. Owens joined her.

"My dear," said that lady, as one who tells good news, " I met that nice Mr. Bell in the post-office and he offered to drive us home in his car. He goes right by our place, you know."

"No!" exclaimed the good little sport, shaking her head resolutely. "I'm going to drive Dandy. You go with him if you'd rather."

For a long moment Mrs. Owens stared at her, as though she were seeing a new Annette, one that she had never known before; a very different Annette from the one that she had brought to the Oaks a few weeks ago. Then she said sighing, " Of course I'll go with you; but, my child, do you think it is exactly safe? "

" No, I don't," was the amazing reply. " Not exactly; still I'm going."

They both went home behind a perfectly behaved pony who was busily engaged in deciding just how many lumps of sugar were his by right for being such a good little pony. He got them too, for when he whinnied and rubbed his soft nose on Annette's sleeve, the little girl found it impossible to harden her heart against the sinner. She even laughed as she went to fetch the sugar bowl.

CHAPTER IX

At the Stable

THE five little Martins were high up in the Elegant Tree.

Here and there among the fluttering leaves there appeared a face; voices called to one another — to Milt upon the very topmost limb, — to Rob climbing as fast as he could to reach him, — to Sarah and Martie curled up in their favorite seats, — to Pigeon busily making a crown of satiny green.

It was late afternoon. Already long shadows were stealing over the little pond while the Elegant Tree, swaying tenderly above it, whispered a good night which was answered by the lap, lap of the tiny waves beneath. There, in the sweet smelling woods beyond, the katy-dids and crickets were having things their own way.

"Katy-did!" shrilled the noisy creatures.

"Katy-didn't!" laughed Milton. "She didn't — she didn't — she did not, I tell you! Katy did not!"

"Katy-did!—Katy-did!—Katy-did!" he was answered from a dozen trees.

"You win," laughed the boy. "She did. Katy did so."

Martie put her fingers to her ears. "Milt, you are worse than they are; do hush. I'm hungry; what about the rest of you?"

Pigeon called out: "Oh, do wait till I finish my wreath."

Sarah asked: "When will Mother and Father be back do you s'pose?"

"Not till late," Martie answered. "Mother said not to sit up for them. Have you most finished, Pigeon?"

Pigeon nodded and placed the green wreath upon her brown head. "Look at me, folks, don't you think I'm just grand?"

"Make it snappy, Mary Ann!" they shouted, as they came trooping up the steps of the Martin House a little later. "We're hungry as tigers."

"And when is it yo're not?" was the answer.

It seemed hours after they had gone to bed that Pigeon saw the light.

She had gone straight to sleep the moment her head touched the pillow, and the next thing she knew she had awakened suddenly, with the room as bright as day.

"I guess it's the moon," she thought drowsily, and then: "My goodness, what's that noise?"

She sat up in bed, the room was brighter than she ever remembered the moon making it, and there was the most dreadful racket going on outside.

"Martie!" she called. "Martie! wake up! What do you s'pose it is?"

It was Milt, however, and not Martie who answered. The two boys were on the sleeping porch which opened from the nursery where Sarah slept with Pigeon.

"That you, Pigeon? I say what's the matter; what's all the fuss?"

She answered: "I don't know. Oh, Milt! listen, there it is again!"

She heard Milton bound out of bed, heard his bare feet upon the floor as he ran to the window; then his voice raised in excitement, shouting:

"The stable's on fire! The stable's on fire, Pigeon! That's Bill braying!"

"O — h!"

She was out of bed and had run to the window. The barn couldn't be seen from the window but the grounds were as bright as day, there was a red glow over everything. Out on the sleeping porch she could hear Milt putting on his shoes.

"I can't make Rob wake up!" he called to her. "And I can't stop. You wake up the others, Pigeon."

Frightened she cried out: "What are you going to do, Milt? Oh, Milt, what are you going to do?"

He answered: "Why get 'em out, of course, Dandy and Bill."

She ran to him and caught hold of his pajama jacket: "Milt, you mustn't! You'll get hurt!"

He cried as he shook off her hand and stood up: " I've got to, Pigeon, I tell you! I've got to!"

"Where's James? Oh, Milt, don't go! Please don't go, Milt!"

She was in tears as she tried to catch hold of him and hold him back, but he slid from her grasp and made for the door.

"I've got to! I tell you, Pigeon, I've got to get 'em out! James isn't here. Don't try to stop me. I tell you I've got to go!"

He had gone flying down the stairs. Clad only in his night clothes and shoes he was hurrying through the hall; and she heard him opening the door. Then she ran to awaken the others.

"Rob! Rob! do wake up! The stable's on fire and Milt has gone. He'll be hurt I know he will! I tried to make him stay, but he wouldn't. . . . He's gone! He's gone to get Dandy and Bill out! Martie! Sarah! Do wake up! The stable's on fire, and Milt has gone!"

Rob, awakened from a deep sleep, sat up and rubbed his eyes. Sarah began at once to ask questions; but Martie slid quickly out of bed without a word. She was wide awake in an instant and tugging at her kimono. Upon her feet were the pink mules which went with it.

"I must go to Milt," she said, as she ran quickly from the room.

"Where's James?" Sarah asked. "Does Mary Ann know? I wonder if Father and Mother have come? Did anyone go to see?"

"I will," Pigeon cried, and raced across the hall. In a moment she was back. Their parents were still away; the room was empty. Mary Ann slept at the far end of the house.

Rob had slipped an old rain coat over his pajamas.

"Old Sallie and her pups are in there too. James put 'em in the stable so he could clean the kennel. Where is James?"

Pigeon answered miserably: "Oh, don't you remember Father said that he could have the day off; that he needn't come back 'till tomorrow?"

Across the lawn, lighted on every side by the dull, red glow from the stable, rushed Milton. Raising his voice he called:

"I'm coming! I'm coming! Dandy! Bill! Sallie! I'm coming! I'll get you out! I'll get you out!"

Remembering that he had read that in a time of fire often horses could not be led to a place of safety unless their eyes were blindfolded, he had snatched at a sweater as he ran through the hall and now he made for the faucet nearest the stable. He turned on the water and held the sweater under it until it was soaked through and through. He must rescue them; good little Dandy and the gypsy mule, and Sallie. He must rescue them somehow, he must!

But how? Before the stable door Milton paused dismayed. From within there came the sound of fire roaring madly, the deep terrified braying of old Bill, the whinnying of the pony calling to his friends, the pitiful howl of Sallie shut in with her babies, — the pretty, helpless, soft, little balls of satin. They were all there, all trusting to him. Reaching up he fumbled with the heavy bar across the stable door. It took all of his strength to lift it and to fling wide the door. So great was the rush of smoke that poured out to meet him that he staggered back, gasping for breath.

"Milt! Oh, Milt! Come back! Don't go in, please, Milt!"

Martie came running towards him; her eyes were wide and frightened. He tried to say, "I've got to, Martie"; but he couldn't speak, he could only look at her and shake his head. He ran into the stable, making his way toward Dandy's stall. The little pony recognized him and whinnied loudly, with delight. All a-quiver with excitement and trembling with fear the gallant little creature waited for someone to come to his help, trusting that the friends who had never failed him would come to him now.

The old building, which had been built by the

children's great grandfather, burned like kindling wood. Dancing, darting flames of fire, crackling, blazing, hissing; every inch of the ancient stable was burning.

Milton, reaching for the pony's head, turned quickly and with Dandy beside him ran to the open door. Once there he turned the pony over to the others; for they were all there now, crowding about the door, calling to him, entreating him to come out, to stay with them.

"Sallie and the babies," he cried quickly, and was gone before they could stop him. Back in the smoke he was searching for them, when he heard a low whine and Sallie sprang upon him, reaching up to lick his face.

Down upon his knees went Milton, feeling about in the straw until his hand touched a soft, sprawly body and, one by one, he gathered up Sallie's four babies and made for the door, with the old setter bounding on in front, making little whimpering noises; her brown eyes big with fear, but trusting for all that — good old dog.

Air and safety.

"Milt! darling Milt, don't go back! Stay with us Milt!"

His twin was at the door, reaching for the pups, begging, beseeching, imploring. "Listen to me, Milt, please! Oh, Milt, listen!"

He must go back. There was Bill still to be rescued. He couldn't, he just couldn't go back on old Bill. Poor old Bill who was making such a racket, who was trying to tell them that things were all wrong; Bill who was calling to them in his distress; begging them to come to him. No, he couldn't go back on Bill, it wasn't to be thought of for a moment.

Mary Ann had awakened by now. She was calling, waving to them, screaming at them from the window in Martie's room; then she was running across the grass, calling to them. Her voice, sharp and frightened, rose high and shrill as she ran.

"Get back! Get back!" she cried. "Get back all of you! . . . Get away, I tell you! Get away from that door!"

"Let me go this time; let me!" Rob was ready to dash in, had not his brother pushed him back.

"No, Rob, no, I tell you. I'm the oldest . . . it's up to me."

He was gone again; back into that furnace of heat and smoke.

Too terrified to move or speak, they huddled there together watching Milt as he made his stumbling way into the stable; then Mary Ann seized hold of them and bore them back away from the door.

"Where's Milt? Where's Milt?" She kept asking.

They could only point. Their tongues refused utterly to move to utter the dreadful words which would tell her that their brother was in the stable; in there with all the flames and fire. Milt was in there — somewhere. She understood without words and running to the stable door she lifted up her voice in a long, beseeching call:

"Milt! Milt! Come back, Milt! Come back! Come back, honey! Come back to yo' Mary Ann, boy! Please, please come back!"

There was no answer.

Inside the stable Milton could hear nothing for the noise of the fire and the deep, frantic braying of the mule shut out all other sounds. Stumbling, fighting, sobbing for breath, he made his way, step by step, toward the stall where the gypsy mule stood.

His eyes smarted; down his cheeks the big, hot tears rolled. Above his head the rafters burned steadily, the flames sweeping upward toward the roof like a crimson curtain. He wanted, he wanted terribly to turn and run back, but he did not. He kept on somehow. On and on until his outstretched hand touched the door to the mule's stall.

With a little cry he drew back. It was so hot that it burnt him.

Again he tried to find the latch, fumbled with it and finally succeeded in opening the door. There he stood, his hand on the big, gray animal which seemed, in the sullen red glow, to tower high above his head like one of the steeds in the

Arabian nights. Somehow he must manage to climb upon his back. Suppose . . . Oh, suppose that he should refuse to move as he had refused that other time.

The boy swallowed hard; then with a rush he was upon the creature's back and holding tightly to his mane. Oh, if James were only here to help! Why had it happened on this night of all nights when his father was away! All about him little angry tongues of flame were darting, now this way, now that. There was a crackling, a hissing; then a dull thud, as a blazing rafter fell across the doorway. The roof of the stable burst into a sheet of flame. If they were to get out in time they must hurry. Milton dug his heels into the sides of the mule, his voice was hoarse as he shouted:

"Go! Bill! Go!"

And Bill went.

As though shot from a cannon that old gypsy mule reared himself for a single second upon shaking hind legs and then he plunged, straight for the stable door. There for a moment he paused in terror of that burning beam which blocked his way; then with a bray of defiance he gathered himself together and leaped clear of it and out to safety.

Those in the racing automobile which sped at top speed up the driveway will never forget the picture of that old gray mule with the small blackened figure upon his back. They saw it first framed against a background of fire; saw it rise in the air and burst out of the door; across the lawn, as though once started it could not stop; saw Milt lift a smudgy hand in greeting; saw his bright head shining like a crown of gold. With a cry of thanksgiving they followed him.

"Milton! Milton! My boy! . . . Oh, my little boy!"

"It's all right, Mother. I'm not hurt a bit."

"But you might have been."

"My son!"

"They are all out, Father, and say, wasn't Bill fine?"

"Someone else was rather splendid too!"

His father's hand was on his shoulder, his father's eyes were proud.

"Hurrah for Milt! Three cheers for Milt! Hurrah!"

Three little Martins were cheering themselves hoarse and as for the fourth little Martin she could only hold fast to that smoke stained jacket as though she could never let it go. What the other twin had suffered during those moments of waiting, they all knew.

"Martie, Martie, old thing, don't cry! I say, it's all right now, Martie; everything's all right." The singed head was very close to the golden one.

"Milt! Milt Martin! Sakes alive, look at him!

Lawdy, what'll that boy do next? " It was Mary Ann, the great tears rolling down her fat cheeks.

" How 'bout that gypsy mule now, Mary Ann? Didn't I tell you he was some mule; didn't I? "

Mary Ann gathered him to her ample bosom.

" I ain't ever goin' to say another word against that old mule. When I looked up and seen him comin' like a race horse with Milt here on his back, I could have hugged him, I could, bones and all! That old mule can have everything he's a mind to ask for; that old gypsy mule sure can! "

CHAPTER X

Sarah Shows Jimmie

ARM in arm with her dear friend Sallie Bell French, Pigeon was strolling home from school.

Although it was just the loveliest kind of a day, neither little girl was looking particularly happy. The third grade had received a blow that morning and the two were deep in a discussion of things at school.

"I don't, for the life of me, see how the third grade is going to get along." Sallie Bell's tone was gloomy in the extreme.

"No," Pigeon wailed, in a voice which matched Sallie Bell's own, "neither do I. Oh, why did Miss Henderson's mother have to go and get sick? Why does Miss Henderson have to go away? Why do things, dreadful things, like this have to go and happen?"

Sallie Bell said, "Don't ask me. There's something I do know though, and that is, I'm not going to like this new teacher. I know I'm not."

The smaller girl stood stock still to stare at her friend.

"Do you feel that way too, Sallie Bell?" she asked. "Well that's ex-act-ly the way I feel about the new teacher. I knew right off, soon as I knew she was coming, I wasn't going to like her, not one bit."

Sallie Bell nodded.

"Let's go home by the little path, Pigeon; I don't want anyone to see me just now. Is my nose very red?"

"It's a good deal red," her companion told her truthfully.

"So's yours. We don't care though, do we?"

The little path was a favorite walk with the two friends. Leaving the main road it went twisting and winding itself among the tall pines. Under foot there was a soft, brown carpet of pine straw, overhead there was stretched a green canopy, through which one could catch a glimpse of the sky.

"I'm feeling better," said Sallie Bell presently.

"It's the little path," declared Pigeon. "So sweet and comforting. Shall I tell you a secret, Sallie Bell? Cross your heart and promise you won't tell."

"Cross-my-heart-and-hope-I-may-die-if-I-do!" was the answer. "Now go ahead and tell me. What's the secret, Pigeon?"

Pigeon told her shyly. "Some day, Sallie Bell, I'm going to write a book and put the little path in it; the little path and all the things I like best."

" What kind of things? "

" Oh, let's see; the garden when it's asleep in the afternoon in the summer time with all the flowers nodding in the sunshine; our pond with the Kiddie Kar bouncing up and down; the Elegant Tree and things like that; I'm going to put them all in my book."

Sallie Bell was staring at her. " My sakes alive, Pigeon Martin," she exclaimed. " Do you s'pose anybody'd want to read a book like that? Do you s'pose they would? "

" I don't care," the little girl cried. " I don't care if anybody reads my book or not, I want them, — the Elegant Tree, the pond, the little path; I want them everyone in my book, I do."

At the Martin House Rob and Jimmie Adkins were out in the garage having a look at the new car. It was a present from their father; a birthday present to their mother, and it had arrived only the day before.

" My aunt! say, it's a peach all right! " Jimmie ran his hand admiringly along the shining side. " Gee, I just bet it can go! I just bet it can, Rob."

Rob Martin nodded as he glanced proudly upon polished wood and glittering nickel. " All to the good, you bet. Just wait till Father runs off the mileage and let's it out, Oh boy! "

Jimmie opened one of the rear doors and put his head inside. " Pretty much all right," was his comment. "Say, let's get in and pretend we're going on a trip, to — a — where'll we go, Rob? "

"Aw, most anywhere," was the answer as they climbed in at the back and settled themselves upon the luxuriant cushions. "Let's go a long way; let's go way out to California, maybe."

"Sure," agreed his chum. "California'll be all right. What's this little shiny thing for? "

Rob explained; "That's where you put your visiting card, if you have any; and this is for smokes and this is — "

He was interrupted by the sound of voices. Sarah, with her arm about Annette Curtis, was passing the garage on the way to the Elegant Tree. Each girl carried a book in her hand, and Annette was walking without her crutch. There was only a slight limp to show which leg had been broken. The little girl spent much of her time at the Martin House with Martie, but today Martie was having a music lesson and Sarah was acting as hostess instead.

The boys whistled to attract their attention. "Hey there," Jimmie called when they had turned and seen them. "Want to come along? We're leavin' in a minute for California. Maybe, if you'll behave good, we'll take you along too."

Sarah answered airily: "Don't bother; we're going ourselves, only we prefer to fly. Our plane is over there," and she waved her hand toward the garden. Then, with the air of having put something over on the two boys, the girls came sauntering in at the wide open door.

Annette asked: " If you are leaving so soon for California what are you doing there on the back seat? "

" You don't suppose," Rob answered, " that we're goin' to drive ourselves. Not much. Jimmie and I don't do things that way. . . . We are waiting for our chauffeur."

The two little girls giggled and climbed into the front seat. Sarah said:

" If we happen to decide not to fly, I might consent to chauffeur you boys. I can run this car as easy as anything."

" Yes you can," scoffed Jimmie. " Run it into the ditch you mean."

Sarah gave him a glance that was intended to wither him upon the spot; a glance which failed of its purpose however.

" I can so! " she cried, " so there! "

" Tell it to the Marines," was the incredulous answer.

" Well I can; I don't care what you say, Jimmie Adkins."

" Like smoke you can: You couldn't run a baby carriage. For a bent penny you'd run it into the ditch, you would."

" That's all you know about it, Mr. Smarty. Last night I was on the front seat when Father was showing Mother. Father said it was just as easy as anything; a baby could run it."

" Oh, sugar, I'd like to see one try."

" Well I could anyway," declared Sarah. " See, this is the self-starter; you just put your foot on it — so. And this is the place you give it gas; this is the — the — well anyway I could run it; it doesn't matter what you say, old Mr. Jimmie Adkins."

" I'd like to see you do it. I guess you're not so smart as you think."

Jimmie's tone was doubting, unbelieving in the extreme. Sarah's eyes flashed fire.

"Well then, Mr. Smarty," she said. " I'll just show you."

Before any of them knew what she was about to do, almost before she knew herself, she had set the gears, there was a click, a purring sound as the engine obeyed, and the big car rolled, quietly and smoothly out of the garage door and onto the driveway.

For a moment none of them made a sound, so utterly amazed were they, then Rob cried out:

" Sarah, are you crazy? What will Father say? "

Twin dimples were in Sarah Martin's cheek, the light of adventure was in her eyes as under her two small hands the great car sped down the driveway toward the gates at the far end, which stood invitingly open.

This was the very most thrilling thing that she had ever done, by far the most delightful; besides wasn't she showing Jimmie? Wasn't she making Jimmie Adkins eat his words? Jimmie would never be able to crow over her again.

"Stop, Sarah!" exclaimed Annette. "Oh! do stop. Don't you see how near the gates we are? You mustn't, oh, you mustn't go out on the road!"

"Sarah Martin, have you lost your senses? Stop this car," exclaimed her brother sternly. "Stop it, I say, this minute!"

They were gathering speed as they glided down the sloping drive, gathering it with every revolution of the wheels.

"You nut, you!" squealed Jimmie. "You crazy little nut, you. Quit tryin' to show off! You'll break all our necks, you will!"

Sarah called exultantly over her shoulder:

"Who said I couldn't run this car? Who said I couldn't?"

They were out of the gates. Out on the open road and still going.

"Stop it!" protested Rob. "Stop it this minute, there's a curve ahead. Stop it, Sarah, you've got to! Quick now!"

Sarah leaned over the steering wheel. The dimples were gone. All of a sudden she was realizing something and that was that she couldn't, that she didn't know how, to stop.

"Stop! stop!" they shouted in her ear. "Stop! Sarah, stop the car!"

"I — I — can't," she answered, almost in a whisper. "I — I don't know how!"

"You've got to!" yelled Jimmie. "We'll all be killed! Stop it, I tell you, stop it."

"I'm trying," she told him, "but everything I do makes it worse!"

"Choke the engine! Do something!" Rob was trying to climb over the seat, his voice was shrill. Annette had covered her face with both hands, while Jimmie, quite purple in the face from shouting orders, was gesticulating with both hands at something approaching from behind at a rapid race.

"It's — it's a motorcycle cop," he gasped. "He's goin' to put us all in jail, and it's all your fault, Sarah Martin."

The motorcycle cop came noisily up from behind and in another moment was abreast of them. He was about to pass when suddenly he turned and glanced quickly at the occupants of the car, who were reduced to silence by Jimmie's startling words.

"Stop!"

His words cut the air like a knife, his uplifted hand was even more commanding; but the big car did not stop, nor did it even slow down. Its speed increased.

"Oh, golly!" groaned Jimmie Adkins.

" We're in for it now; he's a-goin' to put us in jail sho 'nough now."

" Stop! " shouted the traffic policeman. " Stop your car! "

On and on they went never heeding.

The motorcycle shot ahead of them, slowed almost to a stop and, as they came abreast, the rider kicked free his legs, shutting off the engine of the cycle, which fell with a bang to the road. He sprang on the running board and reaching over the side, he soon brought the big car to a complete stop.

" Well! " inquired the voice of the law sternly, " What does this mean? "

Utter silence met his question. The children's tongues seemed to cling to the roof of their mouths. No words came, struggle as they would. It was Rob who managed to speak at last in a voice very unlike his own.

" We — we were t-taking a — a little ride, Mr. Officer. We — "

" So I see," was the disconcerting answer. " And what do you mean by driving a car when you are not of age, young lady? "

He addressed Sarah who could only sit and stare. Her face seemed all eyes, big, astonished, not-too-happy eyes at that.

Her brother came gallantly to her defense.

" She didn't mean any harm, Mr. — Captain, sir. She was just showing us she could run a car."

"I said she couldn't," piped Jimmie. "And she said she could too, and — and I guess she wanted to stop, but — "

"It was a dangerous piece of mischief, young man," interrupted the policeman severely. "Suppose I had not come along when I did, what would you have done? Suppose another car had come around that bend there, how would you have got out of the way of it?"

There was no answer.

He climbed in and, taking the wheel, began to back until they reached the place where he had left his motorcycle.

"Get out," he said to Rob and Jimmie, "and lean that motorcycle against a tree. I'm going to drive you home, and someone there will have to bring me back."

The two boys scrambled out with alacrity, anxious not to offend by being slow. Annette asked in a timid voice, gazing beseechingly into the stern face under the brown cap:

"You aren't going to put us in jail, are you?"

"I should," was the answer. "One can't break the law, you know, and get by with it."

"Oh!" she said, clasping her hands. "Shall we have to stay years and years?"

Her voice was so horror-stricken that the officer's softened somewhat. He said a little less sternly:

"You are rather young, all of you, to begin to

break laws. It was a dangerous, silly thing to do besides. I'm not so sure that I hadn't better take you in to the judge, and see what he has to say about little girls and boys who go joy riding without asking permission."

A faint little voice answered him.

" Don't take them all to — to jail," said Sarah. " It — it wasn't their fault; it — it was all mine!"

" Don't you go listenin' to her, Mr. Officer," cried Jimmie, who had overheard. " She's just a talkin' up a tree, she is. I guess if you take her you'll have to take us boys too. You can let Annette go; she's dreadful scary anyway."

Annette drew a long breath.

" Of course I'll go," she said. Her eyes flashed at Jimmie. " Did you think I wouldn't? " she asked.

Rob, who had returned from placing the motorcycle, spoke quietly, but firmly, looking the officer straight in the eye.

" I'm the one to go," he told him. " I'm a boy and her brother. Take me, won't you please sir, and let the others go along home. Jimmie can go if you say so, but, please, not the girls."

The officer smiled. It was the first time he had done so.

" Get in," he said to Rob. " Tell me where you live. I've got to be moving; and listen to me. I'm not going to take you to jail or anywhere else;

I never intended to; but you've got to give me your word of honor never to try a stunt like this again."

"We won't," they answered solemnly. "We promise."

"No monkey business now. You're none of you to try to run a car till the law says you can; which," he took a long look at them, "will be quite a number of years, if you ask me. Now where's home?"

In five minutes time James was on his way back with the traffic officer in the car, while the four children stood and watched them out of sight; glad to have their feet firmly planted on the ground once more.

Jimmie turned to Sarah:

"Can you run a car, Sarah Martin?" he asked. "Say, can you?"

And that young lady made answer promptly, eating her slice of humble pie then and there:

"No, Jimmie, I can't."

Something in her face made the small boy hasten to say: "Aw, Sarah, don't you feel so badly 'bout it. We're all here, aren't we? The car isn't hurt or anything, and 'sides, you did run it quite a ways, you did."

"I don't want to run it any more," she made answer.

"Come on, folks," said Rob, "Let's go along down to the old Elegant Tree."

Without speaking they sauntered away in that direction. Presently Jimmie Adkins exclaimed:

"When I'm a man, I believe I'll be a traffic cop."

"If you are," said Annette, "I hope you'll be as nice a one as the one who found us."

"Sure," was the reply. "That's the kind I'll be. Gee but it's nice to see the old Elegant Tree again!"

CHAPTER XI

Wild Indians

"HI! Chief! Say, what'll I do with these?"

The small Indian, who had struggled up the hill with both arms filled with packages, stood before the door of the tent. Within the chief was extremely busy with bow and arrow and such things, but he now paused to inspect the splendid feathers that adorned the somewhat moist brow of the young brave before him.

"Gee, Jimmie, but those feathers are the berries all right. I'll say they are. Where'd you get 'em anyway?"

Removing his headgear the better to admire it himself, Jimmie Adkins explained proudly:

"Pretty fine, aren't they? My mother made 'em for me. Say, Milt, you remember that old rooster belongin' to us, don't you? The one that used to go struttin' 'bout so high and mighty? Well, the other day we had him for dinner; had to cook him most a week to get him tender 'nough to eat. Well, these are that old rooster's feathers, dyed, you know. Some feathers I'll say!"

"Sure are," nodded the chief, gazing somewhat enviously, it must be confessed, upon the gaily colored plumage. " They're the best we have in camp. I wish I'd had a rooster. Gosh, Jimmie, but you're lucky all right."

The small boy answered, " Yeah," and asked, " Where're the folks? "

Instantly the chief was the chief. " Heap Indian mighty busy," he explained. " Much work get camp all ready. Why you so late? " accusingly.

The small Indian dug one toe into the sand as he answered: " Just stopped to see if there was any old fish in the brook down yonder. We might need 'em, maybe."

The chief shook his head and answered sternly: " Plenty eat here," he said. " Not plenty work yet. You go get heap busy. Deerfoot and squaws work hard gettin' camp ready while you loaf on job lookin' for fish. Heap poor Injun you."

" Say, I won't loaf another time," promised the very young brave contritely, stooping for the headgear he had placed upon the ground.

The chief stretched out a hand to stop him. " Leave off the feathers now; we've got to get busy gettin' things ready, then we'll dress up and act like Injuns and all. See? "

Redfox saw. The appearance of his chief proved beyond a doubt that he was no loafer. About his bare brown neck little drops of perspiration stood out; while his shining hair clung damply to his forehead. " Hustle along," he directed, " and help get those baskets and boxes unpacked. Say, why did you leave Tige behind?"

"He's comin' along with my mother after awhile," was the answer. "She's a-goin' to bring along a lot of stuff to make lemonade with. I left Tige to sort of take care of her. Gee, but that lemonade sure will taste good, won't it?"

"I'll say," came the appreciative answer.

"Where's that hammock goin'?"

"Between those two big old trees there. It's for Annette mostly."

"She don't need a hammock now."

"Mother thought maybe, every now and then, she might. We can all use it."

"Sure."

"It's going to be a swell camp all right."

"You bet you."

"Say, Jimmie, here's the peace pipe."

He produced a long stemmed pipe from the box he was unpacking, holding it up for the other to see. "Some pipe this."

"What you goin' do with it?"

"Why sit round the fire and smoke the peace pipe, of course."

"What for a peace pipe? I thought we was goin' to fight. I thought we was goin' to be regular fightin' Injuns; and here yo' go talkin' 'bout an old peace pipe and such like. I thought we was goin' on the war path and all that. It isn't a bit of fun bein' peaceful Injuns."

"Why sure we are going to fight," the chief answered. "We are the very fiercest Indians of any there is; but we can't fight every minute. Besides, we ought to smoke a peace pipe sometimes; all Indians do."

"Well I don't want to smoke any old peace pipe," Jimmie exclaimed disgustedly. "I didn't come here to smoke an old pipe like that. I want to paint my face, and put on my feathers and go out and fight and take a whole lot of scalps. That's the kind of Injun I want to be."

There was a shout from the three squaws busily engaged in gathering bits of wood and brush with which to make the camp fire that evening. The two at the tent turned to look. There, coming across the country were several small figures gorgeously attired in full Indian array, with feathers almost, if not quite, as splendid as those of the young brave Redfox.

"Say, who're those Injuns?" Jimmie inquired. "Are they comin' here to play with us?"

The chief nodded.

"Sure they are. It's Ted Rankin, Sallie Bell and Myrtle. Ted's name is Splitmoon. Here comes Annette too."

"Hu," grunted Redfox. "Too many squaws in this camp to suit me."

"Squaws are all right," his chief replied reprovingly. "Squaws do plenty much work, keep camp going while braves are on the war path. Plenty squaws heap good all right."

The plan of setting up an Indian camp was the chief's own idea. Having just finished a story on the life of the Indian, he was eager to become for awhile a red man, and to live for himself all that had so fired his young imagination in the story. He was all Indian just now, aflame with enthusiastic planning for the day, which had begun very early in the morning, as early as they had awakened, and was to continue until after night fall. Their parents had agreed to the plan, with the proviso that James should come in the evening with the car, in which they were to be conveyed home later, and keep a watchful eye upon the fire (which, by the way, was on no account to be lighted until after his arrival upon the scene) from a safe distance, so as not to intrude upon the activities of the red men of the forest. To this they had agreed readily enough, and from that moment plans had gone ahead swiftly and joyously for the great day itself.

The grove, which belonged to the Oaks estate, had been selected as the most likely place in which to pitch the tent. After an early breakfast the children had set out from the Martin House to be joined later by their friends, who were also to become Indians for the day.

A long, happy riotous day in the grove, with an evening thrown in for good measure. Oh, joy!

Time in which to do every one of the exciting things they had heard or read of the Indians doing. No wonder they were thrilled.

Time to hunt the buffalo which roamed at will. Time to sally forth and attack the peaceful homes of settlers and capture prisoners; — taking many scalps. Through the peaceful grove would sound the cry of the red man upon the war path; from behind trees you might see him lurking with painted countenance; slipping from tree to tree so noiseless that his approach was not so much as the snapping of a twig underfoot. Young braves would that day perform deeds of valor, bearing pain without flinching. The chief himself would lead them, while from his lips poured words of wisdom. As for the squaws there was much for them to do — there was food to be made ready against the return of their men; great hunks of the venison slain the day before (cold tongue and chicken must do for this); fish from the stream and sometimes a wild turkey with the arrow still among its feathers. They must fetch and carry at the bidding of their lords without a murmur. Here, however, one of them refused in no uncertain terms the part assigned her. Sarah Martin declared firmly so that all might hear:

"I don't want to be any old squaw, if I've got to be waitin' all the time on men Injuns. I'm goin' to be an Injun brave and do things with some fun to them, I am."

505

"But you can't be a brave, Sarah," objected the chief. "Girls can't be braves. Whoever heard of a girl being an Indian brave."

"I'd like to know why not," exclaimed his sister. "Haven't I got on knickers same as you? Can't I run as fast? And do I cry when I get all scratched up in the bushes? You know I don't. I want to scalp folks and burn 'em at the stake and all that, same as you boys do. Yes, sir, I'm a-goin' to be a brave. I'm tired and sick of being an old squaw. I'm a brave, I am, and my name is Painted Arrow."

"But you haven't any feathers," Jimmie told her.

"That's all you know 'bout it," came the withering reply. "I decided I'd be a brave last night and I went out to the chicken house and got me most enough feathers; if I stick 'em wide apart they'll do."

"Oh!" cried out the gentle Martie, "How'd you get 'em, Sarah? You didn't pull 'em out of the poor hens, did you?"

"Well it didn't hurt 'em," was the quick answer. "Some of 'em just squawked a little, and made an awful fuss flapping round."

"Oh, Sarah, how could you! It was 'most like scalping someone." Martie's blue eyes were troubled.

"How could you see to get 'em?" Rob wanted to know.

"Easy," was the answer. "I took along the big flash light. I took mostly the white ones, cause I could find them better. Course I didn't hurt 'em any, Martie. They've got so many feathers it wouldn't matter to lose a few. Silly things though; you'd have thought I was murderin' them, the fuss they made."

"It's a wonder someone didn't hear and come to see what all the racket was about."

"I was scared to death they would. Mary Ann stuck her head out of the kitchen window once, but I kept still till she went away, and she didn't come out to see. She only said: 'Those fool chickens; som'thin' must be after 'em!'"

"Let's see what you have," the chief asked, and they all waited while Sarah produced a paper parcel tied with string which she proceeded to untie. Then she held up before them her trophies of the night, made into a circle of feathers glued on what was once a fairy crown.

"I play like I've worn 'em on the war path so much they've got kinder scarce," she explained, as she set the crown upon her head.

The chief viewed them rather doubtfully for a moment; then he spoke: "I guess maybe we'll have to let Sarah be a brave, as long as she's gone and got the feathers," he said. "Only I never saw an Indian with such funny looking feathers."

"If Sarah's a brave, I want to be a brave too," declared Pigeon. "I haven't any feathers, but I could be one that's lost 'em swimming the river or something."

"Shucks, you've got to be the papoose, you have; cause we haven't got a papoose and all Indians have 'em," Jimmie told her.

"I won't — I just won't be a little old papoose, so there!" Pigeon turned on the lordly Redfox a disdainful glance.

"Well you can't go ahead and be a sho 'nough Indian; you're too little; so there!"

"I'm most as big as you are, Mr. Smarty."

"Cut it out," commanded the chief loudly. "I say, you two, quit fussing and listen to me. Am I chief of this tribe or am I not?"

"Sure you are"

"Well then listen, all you Indians," he drew himself up to his full young height and folded his arms, while he surveyed them with proud and haughty mien. Then in more stately language gathered from the book he had been reading, he addressed them:

"Listen, oh, my brothers. Why will you wrangle and make war upon each other, when the life of the Indian lies in peril each moment — each hour. Harken, my people, my brave people, nearer and nearer comes the white man; taking from the Indian that which is his by right; that which his fathers had; taking his land, crowding him back and back away from his happy hunting fields forever. Shall we as braves stand for it, my brothers? Shall we do nothing about it? Shall we allow the white man to take that which is ours by right? — Shall we — "

"I'll say not; let's go ahead and beat 'em up!"

Redfox was upon his feet, brandishing a pasteboard tommyhawk over his head and shouting loudly. He felt that they were getting somewhere at last; the real thrill of the day was beginning.

"Peace, my brother, the time is not yet ripe," was the calm reply. "Let not the forest ring as yet with the war cry. Today let us hunt the buffalo and other animals so that there be plenty of food; then, after we have well eaten, we will go forth to slay, to kill, to avenge!"

There was a moment's stillness as they gazed with admiration upon their Chief who had given them such words of wisdom. When they would have spoken, he held up his hand, and they were silent, waiting.

"Today we will prepare; tomorrow at sunrise we will attack. And may those beware whose path we cross! The white man must go — this land belongs to the red man and the red man will keep it! Come, my braves, let us go out into yonder forest where the mighty buffalo prowl and out upon the plain, which is full of them. Make ready that which is needful in the camp, you squaws, until we return."

"I'm a-going to shoot buffalo." Pigeon was not

to be dissuaded from her purpose even by the chief himself. " I'm not going to just wait; that isn't a bit of fun."

" If Pigeon's going to be a boy Injun I'm going to be one too," declared Sallie Bell; and the two, equipped with bow and arrow set forth at the heels of the not too well pleased braves.

" I don't mind being a squaw," Martie spoke loftily. "Pocahontas was a squaw, and everybody thinks a lot of her."

" 'Course," said Myrtle. "And there was an Indian maid who jumped right over a precipice; I've read about her in a book of poetry. She was awful lovely, it says so in the book."

"And there was Minnehaha too," Annette said. " I'm going to have Minnehaha for my name; it means ' laughing water,' you know."

So the three squaws — for their ranks had been reduced to three — set about to spread the table cloth upon the grass and to open the lunch each one had brought, chattering gaily the while about things not altogether pertaining to Indian life, perhaps.

The four original braves, trailed at a short distance by the two recruits, disappeared into the grove which stretched more than a mile ahead of them. They conversed together in language supposed to be as much like the red man's as possible; they pointed and gesticulated; at times stepping quickly behind a tree, or dropping suddenly upon one knee and raising bow and arrow; then on again, now at a run, now creeping slowly on all fours. Behind them the two small Indians were doing the same. If this was the way an Indian brave behaved, then it behooved them to do accordingly, although it was a trifle hard on one's knees; still it was very exciting.

Major and Sallie were enjoying themselves immensely. Sometimes they followed close upon their masters' heels, at other times they went far afield on their own account. The arrival on the scene of the stately white collie only added to their pleasure. They went forward to meet him joyously, voicing their delight in a series of whines and barks.

" See the big white buffalo! Quick, my braves, we eat of its meat tonight; let fly an arrow."

" Don't you hurt my dog," cautioned Redfox hastily. " Don't you hit him with no arrow, not really."

"Who's going to hurt him? Haven't you been shootin' at Major and old Sallie? " Rob (or Deerfoot) wanted to know. " I guess I don't want my dogs hurt either."

" Silence," hissed the chief. " The village of the white man lies there to the east; they must not know that the red man approaches."

Back at the camp the mother of Redfox, gorgeousness itself in a red and gray blanket with many strings of beads about her throat and moccasins upon her feet, was engaged in helping the squaws to make lemonade.

"Gracious but you do look splendid!" Myrtle exclaimed admiringly, and young Mrs. Adkins laughed as she flung aside her blanket.

"It's almost too hot for this," she said. "I nearly melted coming across country, but I did want to dress up too. This is a jolly spot you have chosen for your camp, and that dug-out place seems just made for the fire this evening. Hand me the sugar, please somebody. It's in that brown paper package there. Here, taste it, Martie, and see if you think it's sweet enough. These are the cakes Jimmie left. I'll just rest a moment; then I'll start back. I'm going to do a little fishing after lunch. Tell the young brave Redfox for me, won't you, that his Dad and I will drive over in time to bring him home this evening. His feathers are rather splendid, don't you think?"

The three little squaws exclaimed that they were and politely asked Mrs. Adkins to remain and have lunch with them; an offer which that lady promptly refused.

"Thank you just the same, but I couldn't really. I must run along now. Remember to keep the lemonade covered or some of those flying things will get into it. Well, so long, my dears."

She walked away in the direction of the highway, pausing where the path dipped out of sight to wave a goodbye to them.

" She's nice, isn't she? " said Annette, and the others were about to agree that she was, when the stillness of the forest was broken by a wild and hair-raising screech, the war cry of their tribe. Pigeon's shrill treble rose with the others and echoed through the grove.

" All the same," Martie declared, " I'd rather be a squaw and stay in the wigwam. If they bring home prisoners I shall feel sorry for them, and very probably treat them nicely and maybe help them to escape."

" They'll burn you at the stake if you do," Annette told her, as she tore away the wrapper from a box of crackers. " Oh, goodie, girls, these are just the kind I like."

Then through the grove there came an Indian brave running. From tree to tree he came, pausing to take careful aim every now and then at some unseen foe. Dashing up to where the women of his race were at work, he leaned over to hiss quickly in a whisper.

" I am a wounded brave. I come to bring you a message from the chief. The chief bids me say to you that many villages of the enemy are captured, many are burned; women and children have been taken prisoners; many scalps are ours. Tonight let there be a great feast about the camp fire. Make ready; you have heard the words of the chief. I now go to meet the Great Spirit. Farewell! "

The moist face was serious under its streaks of blue and red crayon; the stern young eyes were unfaltering. He spoke as the chief might have spoken; he knew how to play the game, that was certain, did little Rob Martin; and it was equally certain that he was playing it in earnest. To him the grove was a forest, a forest in which danger lurked for his brother the red man. The white man had proved himself an enemy and, as such, he must be exterminated.

The girls saw him as Deerfoot, as he would have them see him, and not as Rob at all; and seeing him, they knew themselves as Indian maidens, brave and unafraid, maidens who wasted not time in complaining and tears, but who worked swiftly, courageously to do their part. They played the game as he had showed them how it should be played; they ran for water; they opened his buck-skin shirt and staunched the flow of blood which was slowly ebbing; they brought him food and drink and saw him, step by step, recover some of his former strength. The war cry of their tribe rang out again, and they were instantly upon their feet shouting back an answering cry no less fierce. They were Indians in thought, word and deed at that moment.

Home came the victorious tribe to feast in triumph under the shade of the trees; to drink long draughts of the cool lemonade from the white bucket, and to lie back upon the grass when the feast was over, and rest.

"We've got to go and cut down a tree or something to make a stake," said the Chief. "Where's the hatchet?"

"Yeah, and somebody's got to get burnt at that old stake too," added the flushed but happy Redfox. "Somebody sho' has."

"We'll tie Martie and burn her," Deerfoot suggested; but Redfox objected, "Let's burn Annette; cause she'll squeal like anything, same as if she was really bein' burnt, she will. We'll tie her to the stake and hear her yell."

"I won't either!" Annette exclaimed. "I won't cry any more than Martie will. I'll be brave as — as Joan of Arc, and nobody could be braver than she was."

"I bet all the same you just holler and screech when you see the flames," Redfox insisted.

"Flames?"

"Course not real ones, silly; that is not right smack at your feet; but we're goin' to put that stake just as near the camp fire as we can, so it 'twill seem like it was goin' to burn folks up sho 'nough. Aw, gee! I can just hear you a yellin' now."

The finding of something worthy to be called a stake, and the work of getting it ready and set up for the unfortunate victim required a good deal of time. The afternoon waned and the sun sank slowly behind the grove, which was filled with a soft silver radiance, in which the trees rustled and whispered to one another.

Again the warriors went forth to pillage and burn, to take some prisoners, and to scalp others. Once again the stillness of the forest was rent by the fearsome war cry, so shrill, so penetrating. Again the faithful squaws heard, and sent back their own cry to meet it. At dusk they sped triumphantly to the tent and ate hungrily of the lunch which was holding out like the widow's cruse; then pleasantly weary from the long and strenuous day, but quite happy, they gathered about and waited for James to come, that they might light the fire.

The lighting of the fire was the great event of the day, the event to which they had looked forward with the greatest possible anticipation. Outdoor picnics were plentiful in the summer time, but to remain until after dark; to kindle their own fire and in its light to continue this most fascinating of games was something very much out of the ordinary.

The sound of the automobile horn told them that James was approaching; next they saw him come striding through the grove to see that the fire was properly lighted and to caution them as to how near they might approach to it. Then, with a grin at the savage Indians, James tactfully withdrew to a distance, where he could see without being himself in evidence, and the game went on.

First came the burning of Annette at the stake; a flushed, excited rather timid Annette, who squealed as Jimmie had predicted as she was being bound; while they danced about her, waving tommyhawks and shouting in a barbarous tongue. Round and round they went, until their victim was supposed to be consumed by flames, and they themselves worn out by their exertions. Then they were glad to release her and sit down to rest and to smoke the pipe of peace.

Gravely the chief took the long stemmed pipe in his hand. He was just about to place it between his lips, when suddenly it fell to the ground; out from the shadows there had stepped a strange and awesome figure.

It was an Indian in paint and feathers like themselves, except that he towered above them until he seemed as tall as the trees and as straight. From one shoulder there was flung back the end of the splendid blanket that he wore fastened about him, as he stood there with folded arms, gazing at them.

A real Indian — or so he seemed — among the play Indians.

So silently had he come that they had not been aware of his approach until he stood before them.

"My children," he said, "My little children of the forest; I come to give you greeting. I, Rain-in-the-face, chief of the mighty tribe of Iroquois have listened to your war cry this day in the forest. I have heard often of your deeds of valor. Oh, my brothers, I come to sit before your council fire and smoke with you the peace pipe."

Breathlessly they gazed at him, so stern, so splendid, and each small heart beat high with excitement.

He held up his hand for silence, although none of them had moved. They all sat spellbound. "Out of the forest I come to you. My time is short; I have far to go. Three sleeps from this hour I shall be far away, traveling swiftly. Before many moons have waned I shall hunt and fish in a country far away; but some day I shall come again to gather with you about the council fire. It is spoken."

Then arose their chief and facing the stranger, he spoke:

"Smoke, my brother, so that there shall be peace between us."

Reaching out a hand that shook slightly, he took the pipe of peace and placed it between his lips; then without a word he passed it to the strange visitor and he in turn to Redfox and so on around the circle, until each had puffed at the red coal placed so carefully within its bowl, and which still remained.

There was silence; only the wind sighed through the trees above their heads.

"Great and mighty chief," spoke the stranger, breaking the stillness. "Wouldst travel with me many sleeps to the land of the setting sun? Come then, we will break camp and away, for the white man threatens our land and drives away our deer and wild turkey. We will hasten to make our camp beside other waters in a far country. Let us be going, my children; the night wanes."

The tall Indian went striding away and was lost in the dimness of the grove.

"It's just like a story book!" cried Sallie Bell.

"He — he looked like uncle Bob," breathed Pigeon wide-eyed. "Do you s'pose it could have been? My wasn't he splendid!"

Back upon the highway a horn blew, three short blasts and one long one, the signal that the day was over and that Jimmie's father and mother were waiting for him.

Like wild Indians they sprang to their feet and sent an answering whoop through the stillness.

CHAPTER XII

MEASLES

FATHER was going away on a business trip of two weeks and Mother was going with him. There were many things to be said the last minute, just before the long train came puffing up and bore them away.

"You're to have your party, dearest, just the same," Mother told Pigeon. "It wouldn't seem a real birthday without a party. Martie has our presents for you and she will produce them when the great day comes. We'll be thinking of you all day, love, and will send you a birthday telegram, of course. Mary Ann will see that the refreshments are forth-coming as usual. The big box of souvenirs came last week and it's in the closet under the stairs. Have a beautiful time and write us all about everything."

Just planning for the party helped a good deal after Mother and Father were gone. There were games to be thought up, and the kind of little cakes to be decided on, besides the big white birthday cake which Mary Ann always made and which held the place of honor at every little Martin's birthday, with a very specially large one when the twins' turn came. Then there was the list of guests to be made.

"There's Jimmie and Sallie Bell and Myrtle of course," Pigeon sat biting the end of her pencil thoughtfully. "And the two Jones children and, oh, yes, Katie Gray, Betty and — and who else? Come and help me think, Sarah."

With Sarah's help the list was soon complete, and beginning with the next morning Pigeon Martin became quite important in the third grade as one who was about to give a party. She was invited to share lunch with almost every little girl present, while several little boys inquired politely if her pencil needed sharpening. It was all very exciting and delightful, as she confided to Sarah that night, having so many people wanting to do things for you. Sarah, who had also had birthdays, agreed that it was.

It was Rob who cast the first bomb into the party when he announced at dinner one evening, "Jimmie's sick. I was over there this afternoon and Jimmie's mother said Jimmie had a fever and she'd sent for the doctor. I didn't see him; she thought I'd better not."

"Oh, dear," exclaimed Pigeon. "Do you s'pose he'll be well in time for my birthday party? Telephone, Rob, won't you, and see how he is? Tell him to hurry up and get well."

Rob reported when he came from the telephone that Jimmie had the measles; not a very severe case, but enough to keep him in bed for awhile.

Jimmie, so it seemed, had set the ball rolling for the third grade, and they began to go down like tenpins. At first, here and there, about the school room there was an empty desk; then there appeared a whole number of empty desks all of a sudden, until the happy, jolly little third grade was reduced to only a very few, and these might go down at any moment. Miss Henderson, at the first sign of a listless, red-faced little pupil, sent the child home at once with orders not to return until he or she had seen a doctor.

After eight days Jimmie Adkins was back, apparently none the worse for his sickness. His first glance took in the sadly depleted room, and he whispered to Pigeon as he passed her desk:

"Things don't look so hot for the party, do they?"

Pigeon, who was obliged to scratch another name from the rapidly diminishing list each day, shook her head.

At the Martin House Mary Ann was going on with the preparations, just as if no thought of measles threatened the birthday celebration. The little cakes turned out to be gems of deliciousness within their pink and white frostings; the big birthday cake was most certainly a thing of beauty, as it stood with its seven tall candles, one for each of the happy years of the little girl's life, waiting to be lighted the very next afternoon.

The evening before the birthday the telephone was decidedly active. Three times it rang, and each of those calls was for Mary Frances Martin; three times she returned from the hall where the telephone stood looking rather doleful for a little girl who is about to have a birthday; three times she explained to her sympathetic family that someone else couldn't come to her party tomorrow.

"Hard luck, Pigeon, old top," Milt condoled, glancing up from his home work. "We'll eat up the stuff, don't you fret, and have a good time too."

But Pigeon did fret in spite of Milt's cheering advice. She wanted a birthday party, with all the frills that went with it. She wanted the children crowding into the big house; she wanted the fun and excitement of the games; she wanted that altogether thrilling moment when the glass doors leading into the dining room were thrown open by a smiling Mary Ann in a white apron and cap while at the same time a grand march began on the piano. She remembered the long, hilarious processions of former birthdays which had wound themselves noisily through the library, hall and living room on out into the hall again, and from there into the dining room; there to pause with long drawn cries of delight at sight of the table.

She knew exactly what a birthday party should be, did little Mary Frances Martin, and she wanted one just exactly like those she had always had; and now the old measles wasn't going to let her have it. Oh, dear! it was enough to cloud any birthday having things behave like this, with Mother and Father away too.

Early next morning the familiar tinkle of the telephone brought Pigeon bolt upright in bed. "It's somebody else can't come to the party, I know," she wailed to Sarah who had also wakened.

Both little girls listened to the sound of Julia's footsteps going through the hall, and then her voice at the instrument speaking:

"This is Mr. Martin's residence. Mary Frances? No, mam, she isn't down yet. Why, yes mam, I'll give her the message. I know she'll be sorry. Yes, I'll be certain to tell her; goodbye."

" I knew it! I knew it!"

Pigeon lay back on the pillow; she had to blink very hard to keep back the tears which stung her lashes. Sarah, leaning on one elbow, exclaimed: " Don't you dare cry, Pigeon Martin! If you cry on your birthday — if you let a single tear fall that day, you'll have something to cry about every single day of the whole year, 'cause Mary Ann told me so."

" I'm not crying, Sarah." The small girl swallowed bravely and faced her birthday with a resolute air.

" I'll run and wake the others," Sarah told her,

" and we'll begin to celebrate right off, before that old telephone rings another time."

Never was a birthday allowed to pass over the heads of the five little Martins without this celebration in the early morning. It consisted of the ringing of bells, the blowing of combs covered over with tissue paper, the kissing, one kiss for every year, of the person whose birthday it was, and the marching, to the squeak of the combs, down to the dining room, where the gifts had been placed upon the table. The chair of the birthday person was always decorated, and he or she was expected to wear throughout the meal a silver crown, and to answer to the greeting of " Happy birthday to you! " " Let's all of us have a good time."

Sarah seized the comb she had made ready the night before, wrapped the paper about it and blew a frightful blast.

" Wake up, everybody, wake up! It's Pigeon's birthday."

The birthday telegram from Mother and Father came as they were seated about the breakfast table. Pigeon, with the silver crown upon her little brown head, read it aloud. It was a long one, a night letter, and carried to the child the added knowledge of her parents' love and best wishes upon this most happy occasion. It was only at the end that her voice trembled and faltered when they spoke of the birthday party; told her that they would be thinking of her and her little friends, and hoped that everything would go off beautifully.

"If they could see all these cakes," said Pigeon to Sarah, as the two stood in the pantry just before starting off to school, "they'd know that things weren't going off so beautifully; anything but."

Upon the immaculate shelves there stood the little cakes in a solemn row waiting to be eaten and (could anything be sadder) there were but seven children in all to eat them. Upon the shelf above towered the birthday cake in all its grandeur; while in the tall tins were candies of different kinds and colors, and deep yellow bowls held the cream which was to be made into that without which no party is complete, the ice cream.

"Come on," sighed Sarah, whose heart was filled with pity for the disappointment of her small sister, "it's time to start. Anyway, Pigeon, we can be thankful we haven't the measles."

"Yes, I s'pose so," was the rueful reply.

The third grade presented a sorry spectacle indeed that winter's morning, with its rows of vacant desks, and the few small scholars seated there with wide gaps between them. The wise and kind Miss Henderson decided that the remaining few needed the sunshine much more than they did the school room just then, if they were to keep on their feet in the days to follow.

"Run along home, little folk," she told them, "and spend the day out-of-doors. I don't want another case of measles in the third grade. I'm sick of the sight of empty desks. Hurry along all of you and have a good time."

Pigeon and Jimmie hurried out with the others, but as to having a good time, Pigeon wasn't so sure about that.

She sighed a little sigh of disappointment as she passed Sallie Bell's desk and longed for the companionship of Myrtle with all her heart. Both little friends were convalescing from the measles.

"I guess the birthday party's a fizzle," she told Jimmie, as the two trudged the homeward road. "Just a plain flop."

"Heap more ice cream for the rest of us," was that young gentleman's unfeeling retort.

"Pig!"

She tried withering him with a glance, but it was not so easy to disconcert Jimmie. Suddenly he wheeled to face her, his brown eyes as scornful as her own had been a moment before.

"I guess if I had a birthday I just wouldn't go and let it be a flop. No siree bob, I wouldn't! Girls are like that, they are; every little thing just goes and knocks 'em flat, it does."

"But, Jimmie," — Pigeon was too surprised to be angry — "what would you do if it was your birthday and everyone was down with the measles? How can I possibly help it? I'm sure I

don't want my birthday party spoilt any more
than you do, so there! "

" Then why don't you go ahead and do something about it, 'stead of lookin' mournful like —
like our old Whitie? "

" Don't you dare call me a cow, Jimmie Adkins." Pigeon felt that she had taken enough from
Jimmie without this added insult. " I guess you'd
feel plenty mournful too if your birthday party
was spoiled com-plete-ly."

" Then, if you feel that way 'bout it, for Pete's
sake why don't you do somethin'? "

Jimmie fairly hurled the words at her. " Just
sayin' how sorry you are every minute don't help
any; it's just plain silly."

" What can I *do*? "

" I bet I'd find somethin' to do mighty quick
if it was my party."

" Oh, you would, Mr. Know-all? "

" Yes, I would."

" Then s'pose you tell me. Go ahead and tell
me, Jimmie Adkins, just what you'd do if most
all the children you had invited were sick and
couldn't come? "

" I'd ask others, I would."

Pigeon stared at him. " You'd ask other children? Who would you ask? Where would you get
those other children, I'd like to have you tell
me? "

Her companion made an eloquent gesture

which might have included half the children in the universe; "I'd find 'em," he answered, confidently. "You just bet your sweet life, Pigeon Martin, I'd find 'em somewhere."

"Tell me where," begged Pigeon, "and I will."

"Well," the small boy wriggled his freckled nose in an effort to think, he ground the toe of his shoe into the path and rammed both brown fists deep into trouser pockets. It was plain that Jimmie was playing for time and inspiration. The latter came at last, he said carelessly:

"What's the matter with invitin' Joey Hub? I just bet Joey's never been to a birthday party."

Pigeon bet so too. She stared at Jimmie; she must have misunderstood. It couldn't be that he was proposing Joey Hub for her party, not really."

"Joey Hub? Did you say Joey Hub, Jimmie?" she asked.

That young man nodded. "Yeah, that's what I said, Joey Hub. Didn't you ask me to help you? You did, and then the very first crack out the box you look funny and say —"

"But do you think Joey Hub's a nice boy, Jimmie?"

"No, 'course he isn't; whoever said he was? He's the worst boy in the village, everybody says so."

"And still you tell me to invite him to my birthday party?"

"There you go, after last Sunday and everything," Jimmie was scornful in the extreme. "Just like a girl!"

"What's last Sunday got to do with Joey Hub?"

"It's got a lot. Didn't Miss Jones sit up in class and tell us 'bout bein' nice to children who hadn't 'vantages like we have; didn't she? Didn't she say we should help 'em all we could, and give 'em pleasure an' things like that? An' wasn't our lesson 'bout a man who had a party and 'vited people and they wouldn't come? Maybe they had the measles too, it didn't say — "

"It did say," interrupted Pigeon. "It said that one of them — "

"Well they telephoned they weren't comin' any way, didn't they? Yes sir, that's just what they did; but the man didn't sit down and look sick, and say it was too bad, did he? No sir, he didn't. He up and got him some more folks, so the party wouldn't be a fizzle, he did. An' 'cause he had to ask 'em in a hurry he had to get anybody he could. I guess there was a lot of folks there worse'n Joey Hub."

"Maybe," she admitted doubtfully. "Now who else?"

"You want me to do all the work for this old party. Haven't I just named one and you want me to go right ahead an' keep on naming 'em! It's up to you now; you ought to be able to think of someone, goodness knows. You oughtn't to sit back and 'spect me to do all the work, Pigeon."

Pigeon was not listening. She was so used to Jimmie's flying off the handle that she gave him little or no thought.

"Jimmie," she asked suddenly, "there's the O'Briens. You know who I mean?"

Jimmie shook his head.

"They live in that tumble-down house at the edge of the village. Mrs. O'Brien does Mother's curtains for her. I've been there lots of times with Mother, and, Jimmie, they have hundreds of children, I believe."

Jimmie nodded: "What are their names?"

Pigeon shook her head. "Goodness, Jimmie, I don't know; but I do know Mrs. O'Brien, and I guess she knows; we might go and ask her if they can come."

"How many?"

"As many as are big enough. Come on."

They turned about and set their faces resolutely toward the O'Brien home. On the way they passed a tiny cottage where a rather sweet faced woman was sweeping off the porch, while a small boy with bright black eyes was swinging idly on the rickety gate. Jimmie whispered hurriedly:

"That's Joey Hub's mother, and there's Joey. Go ahead and ask him now, why don't you?"

Pigeon drew a long breath, took, as it were, her courage in both hands, and approached the gate which was protesting loudly under the weight of the boy. "How do you do?" she smiled politely while Joey stared at her in amazement, and his mother answered for him, "How do you do yourself, Miss? It's one of the little Martin girls, isn't it?"

"Yes," said Pigeon. "I'm Mary Frances Martin, and — and please, this is my birthday. I'm going to have a party. I — I'd like Joey to come, if he'd like to."

"Who, me?"

Joey Hub let the gate bang to with a force which almost shook it from its hinges forever. Mrs. Hub seized her broom in both hands, as if she needed its assistance to keep her on her feet and her face flushed a quick warm red as she stared at the little girl in the blue tam and coat.

"Yes," Pigeon said to Joey, "wouldn't you like to come to my party?"

"Ma!" shrilled Joey's excited voice, although his mother was but a few paces away, "Ma, she wants me to come to her party!"

Pigeon was embarrassed; she was thankful for Jimmie's presence close beside her. The mother of Joey came down to the gate, the broom still clasped in her hands.

"You want Joey to come to a party at your house?" she inquired, a bit incredulously. "You want my Joey here?"

"She said so," Joey cried out quickly. He had not taken his eyes from Pigeon's face, and he continued to stare at her, as his mother questioned gently:

"Does your mother know that you are asking Joey? Did she say you might?"

"Mother and Father are both away," the little girl answered, adding, "it's all right. Mother said I might invite all of my friends, and now most of them are sick with the measles; so I'm asking others in their place."

"She wants me, Ma."

Mrs. Hub placed a hand on the thin little shoulder under the faded shirt: "Yes, yes, son, that's nice of her. You'd like to go to a real party, wouldn't you, Joey?"

"Sure I'd like to go." Joey Hub was trembling a little, his bright black eyes were brighter than ever. "I'm a-goin', Ma; them pants you'll —"

"I'll get you ready," said his mother kindly. She turned to Pigeon and her voice was eager, and rather wistful: "You won't be ashamed of Joey. When is the party to be?"

"This afternoon," Pigeon answered, "at four;" and then she added, "I'm glad you'll let Joey come, Mrs. Hub."

Joey's mother said, her hand still upon the quivering little shoulder: "Thank you for inviting him, Miss Mary Frances. It was nice in you. You've done a good deal for Joey today."

"Well so-long," piped Jimmie, who had decided that it was about time to be upon their way.

They went along the quiet village street leaving Joey still staring after them. His mother had taken the broom in her hands and was finishing the porch. The flush was still on her cheeks.

The visit at the O'Briens was altogether different.

Mrs. O'Brien greeted her guests with smiles and loud expressions of welcome, while the numerous little O'Briens gathered round to inspect the newcomers.

"Well now, if it ain't Miss Pigeon. Bless your heart, honey, where'd you drop from this foine morning? Sit right down; no, not in that chair, it's a bit off in the legs, you know. Run get another chair, Patsy, and be sure you dust it off."

"We haven't time to sit down," Pigeon interrupted gently but firmly. From previous visits she knew that there was no getting in a word edgewise once that good woman was fairly launched. "We've — this is Jimmie Adkins, — come to invite some of the children to my birthday party this afternoon at four."

"Well now, that's nice of you, for a fact," beamed the pleased mother of the little brood. "And which ones will you be after wanting now? There's Patsy here would admire to go to a party at your house I'm sure. Patsy is home from school for the day; she just came a few moments ago; she — "

"Yes," said Pigeon. "I know. Patsy is in my room at school. Miss Henderson sent us home. Will Patsy come?"

"Will she stay away?" was the laughing answer. "Sure and she'll be there on the stroke of four, she will that. And Micky now, would you be after having Micky come?"

Jimmie gave Pigeon a poke in the ribs. "Hurry and tell her yes," he said, "we haven't all day to stay, Pigeon."

"Yes," replied Pigeon. "I'd like very much to have Micky come, and . . . and are there any more about Patsy's age, Mrs. O'Brien? If there are, I'd like to have them come too."

Mrs. O'Brien laughed delightedly.

"Well I must say that's real handsome of you. 'Tis sitting down I wish you'd be, an' visiting with me awhile. Indeed, there is Katie now, and Nora and Timmy; all of them would admire to come, an' thank you, my dearie, for the wanting of them."

"I'm afraid it will be quite a walk to the Martin House, for some of them," began the small visitor anxiously when, with another laugh, her hostess dispelled all her fears for the small O'Briens.

"Don't you be after worrying about that, bless your heart for the thinking of it just the same;

but 'tis himself who has bought a truck only last week; 'tis the hauling business he is in you see, an' 'twas a truck he was after wanting this long time. And now 'twill come in foine to ride the children to your party, Miss Pigeon; 'twill that."

The little O'Briens thus arranged for, Jimmie and Pigeon moved on. They were passing the window of Miss Molly Bunn's tiny store when the little girl exclaimed:

"I believe I'll go in and ask Miss Molly to come to my party, Jimmie!"

"What for?" demanded her escort. "Why do you want to invite a grown up lady, Pigeon?"

"'Cause I do," was the answer. "She's always so nice, Jimmie; and I believe she'd enjoy cutting the birthday cake and all that. I'm going to ask her and see what she says."

"Well go ahead; it's your funeral," her companion made answer. "I'll wait here while you're gone."

Jimmie was ready for her when she came out of the store a moment or so later, pleased that her friend Miss Molly had consented to leave the little shop in charge of a friend and come to her birthday celebration.

"Dear me, child," she had said, quite in a fluster. "I haven't been to a party in so long I'm afraid I shan't know how to behave. It's sweet of you to want me. I can't wait to see those candles burning on your birthday cake, dear little girl."

"Seems to me," declared Jimmie, "if there's one grown-up a-comin' there ought to be another. One grown-up'll feel mighty lonely. Seems to me you ought to go ahead and ask another, Pigeon."

"Who'll I have for the other?"

"Well, let's see; there's Mr. Hollins. You might have him."

Pigeon nodded. "I might," she answered. "Do you think Mr. Hollins would like to come, Jimmie?"

"Sure he would," with the confident answer. "Come on, let's ask him."

Mr. Hollins, who was an old friend of both children, kept the general store in the village, where anything from a paper of pins to a truck might be purchased; though to the children the most important articles in the entire establishment were the long, pink and white peppermint walking-canes that hung in the glass case. Pigeon was very friendly with Mr. Hollins. She had known him ever since she was a small girl; so small that she had to stand on tiptoe to see above the top of the counter. Mr. Hollins knew all about the party, for it was he who had sent a special order to the city to have the paper caps sent out; and he had brought them to the Martin House himself on their arrival, more than a week ago.

Mr. Hollins was glad to see them. "Well how goes the party?" he inquired of Pigeon, leaning across the counter to smile into the rosy face under the blue tam. "You've got a swell day for it, I must say. Is everything O.K. up at the house?"

The little girl nodded. "Yes, thank you, everything is all right. Jimmie and I came in, not to buy anything this morning, but to give you an invitation."

"Well! well!" exclaimed Mr. Hollins jovially, "that is certainly mighty fine of you and Jimmie. What kind of an invitation is it?"

"I want you to come to my birthday party. It's this afternoon at four o'clock, and I hope you'll come. Jimmie hopes so too, don't you, Jimmie?"

"Sure," agreed that young gentleman, and sauntered away, hands in pockets to have a look at some fishing tackle at the other end of the store.

"Well now," went on the good natured gentleman a trifle taken by surprise. "That is nice; one of the very nicest things I ever heard of. To think of your wanting me, little Miss Mary Frances; an old fellow like me to come to your birthday party."

"But I do want you," Pigeon said. "I want you ever so much. Please come. Miss Molly is coming," she told him. "So you needn't feel lonely at being the only grown-up person there, as maybe you might."

"So Miss Molly's coming is she?" he said,

smiling. "Well, that's nice too. I haven't seen Miss Molly Branch to talk to, in quite a spell now."

"You'll come then," Pigeon said. "At four o'clock; and please come on time, so that we can begin right off to play."

"Eh? what's that?" he exclaimed. "To play? Why of course. That's what people do at parties to be sure. Miss Molly and I'll do that; we'll play 'Ring around the roses,' and such like. Thank you little Miss Mary Frances Martin, count on me. I'll be there!"

"Joey's going to a party," Mrs. Hub told her next door neighbor proudly.

"I'll be right over," called Mrs. Simms, and putting her dinner on the back of the stove where it would not burn, she made haste to gather further information.

"You say Joey's going to a party?" she inquired a moment later, coming in at Mrs. Hub's back door, amazement written largely upon her round face. "How did that happen?"

"It's the little Martin girl," Mrs. Hub explained, as she searched the box where she kept her sewing for a button to sew on the shirt she was mending. "She's going to have a party; it's her birthday; and she wants my Joey."

"Not the little Martins who live in the big house along the road?"

"The same."

Mrs. Hub's eyes were shining; behind her calm exterior her thoughts were running in this wise. " My Joey can't be as bad as people say, or else the little Martin girl wouldn't invite him to her party. My Joey's a better boy than people think. I'm glad for Mrs. Simms to see how much some folks think of Joey. Think of his being invited to a party at the Martin place."

Mrs. Simms' thoughts were also running apace as she sat there rocking back and forth.

" I hope he'll behave," she thought. " I hope he won't be cutting any of his capers and ruining the party for that nice little Martin girl. What ever possessed her to go and ask him anyway? He's sure to do something dreadful before he's through. He's just the very worst boy I ever set eyes on, and goodness knows that's saying a lot."

" Ain't it nice? " Joey's mother was smiling; her face had not lost the flush of pleasure little Mary Frances Martin's words had brought to it.

" Fine," responded her neighbor, not too enthusiastically it must be confessed. She asked: " You're getting him ready; are those the clothes he's going to wear? What time's the party? "

" Four," answered Mrs. Hub. " She said four; it's her birthday."

" How old is she? "

" I dunno; six or maybe seven. She's such a pretty little thing."

" How'd she happen to ask Joey? "

The question had been burning Mrs. Simms' tongue; now it was out at last. Her curiosity had got the better of her manners, she did so want to find out why Joey Hub had been invited. She did not find out, for the reason that Mrs. Hub did not know herself.

"My Joey has wonderfully taking ways with children, Joey has," Mrs. Hub answered proudly, and held up the button she had at last found. "Do you think this will do; it's a little large but —"

"I've got a better one," Mrs. Simms told her, and wondered why she should be giving Joey Hub a button for his shirt; Joey who made her life a burden so often; Joey who was always doing something he shouldn't. "I'll step home and get it," she said, rising from the rocking chair with an effort. "It won't take a second."

As she crossed the tiny bit of yard to her door she said to the old tabby cat dozing on the back fence with the eye toward the Hub house only half closed: "Go ahead and sleep, if you've a mind to. Joey Hub's got some thing better to do today than torment the life out of you. He's going to a party, he is; and the Lord only knows why he was asked!"

"Maybe he does behave sometime," she soliloquized as she searched for the button that she had come after. "Maybe there's some good in him; there ought to be with him havin' such a nice mother."

She found the button and started back. To tabby as she passed she spoke again: "Go on and make the best of it; now's your chance!"

Out into the sunshine Pigeon and Jimmie turned their faces toward home. "I guess that will do," Pigeon exclaimed. "We might squeeze in another, but I think that's enough, don't you, Jimmie?"

Jimmie nodded. "Let's go along home now," he said. "Wonder if Mary Ann's started on the ice cream? I'll run along, have my lunch and come back early. Let's hurry; say it makes folks dreadful hungry to go round 'vitin' people to birthday parties, don't it?"

CHAPTER XIII

The Birthday Party

THE rest of the Martin children were late in coming home after school that day. First one thing and then another had happened to keep them; they arrived at last, however, and came hurrying into the house where Mary Ann, with Julia's help, was busy setting the table in the big dining room.

"Yo' children go on in the breakfast room," she called out to them. "Lunch is on the table a-waitin' for yo'; so hurry up!"

"Where's Pigeon?" they asked.

"Where yo'd better be; upstairs gettin' dressed for her party."

"There's going to be one then?"

"'Course there is; what makes yo' think there isn't?"

"We thought everybody was too sick to come."

"Huh! this don' look much like it," pointing to the long table. "Now yo' all go on and hurry; the company'll be here befo' you get dressed."

"We'll hurry. Have you plenty of ice cream, Mary Ann?"

"Did yo' ever see the time when I didn't?"

was the answer. "Go on, an' quit botherin' me. Don' you see I've got my table to set?"

Up stairs in the nursery a somewhat nervous Mary Frances was getting dressed. She was beginning to ask herself if she had done well to listen to Jimmie. Would her parents approve of the guests she had invited? What would her brothers and sisters say? Even more important, what would Mary Ann think?

Without the stimulus of Jimmie Adkins' uplifting presence these disturbing thoughts were beginning to weigh her down a bit; she was beginning to think that perhaps it would have been better not to have listened to Jimmie and his arguments; best maybe to have had only Jimmie and her brothers and sisters. Well it was done now. She went to the closet, lifted down her pale blue party dress and slipped quickly into it. She felt suddenly that she would rather be down stairs when the others came up to dress; she didn't want to be asked a thousand questions; time enough for that later.

Down in the long living room she waited a little uncertainly. From over the banister Martie called down to her:

"So there's really going to be a party, Pigeon?"

"Yes, there — there's almost as many as Mother said," she answered, wondering if her voice sounded as troubled as she felt.

Evidently not, for Martie answered at once: "That's good. I'm ever so glad, Pigeon."

"Me too," Sarah piped. "I'll be down in a moment."

Milton was the first to arrive on the scene. In white trousers and blue coat he came into the room just as there was a loud noise outside and through the stately gates of the Martin grounds rolled the truck load of radiant, shouting little O'Briens. Running to the window, Milt pulled the curtains aside and looked out; while his sister came to stand beside him. The truck rolled gaily up the driveway to stop before the front veranda with much grinding of brakes and joyful laughter. Behind the O'Briens came a fat man on a bicycle, and trudging in at the further gate was a small boy with his cap pulled low over his eyes. They were all here except Miss Molly, and even at the moment, a taxicab turned in at the gates, passed the boy and sped on up the driveway to come to a stop behind the truck which was unloading its merry passengers. Miss Molly had arrived, and Jimmie, who had come in the back way with his little friends, appeared on the scene at the same moment. All the guests were here.

"Say, is this the party?"

Milt asked it breathlessly and then, at her nod of acquiescence, went forward with her to assist in greeting the guests, like the little gentleman he was.

"There's six O'Briens," whispered Jimmie to Pigeon, "'stead of only five like they said."

There was. Patsy O'Brien explained that at the last moment Danny had seen the others dressing, and had howled so to come that his mother had sent him along with his sisters and brothers.

"Ma said you wouldn't mind," she said. "Ma said as how your house was big enough for us all, and Danny was a-screeching like a house afire so 'fraid he'd be left. That's Micky's shirt he has on, an he's that proud of it! Watch him strut like a turkey gobbler! He's that happy to be here."

"I'm glad he came," Pigeon said, "and won't you please walk in? This is my brother Milton."

Mr. Hollins placed his bicycle beside the veranda step and helped Miss Molly from the taxi. Mr. O'Brien said that he'd be seeing them later, and to be good children and not eat too much. Joey Hub, with his bright black eyes peeping from beneath his cap, came up, rather red of face and out of breath. Rob Martin, who was on his way down stairs, gave a low whistle of surprise and sat down suddenly.

"Hurry up," he called to his sisters. "Pigeon's party's on."

They went into the big living room, after leaving their wraps in the hall, where an open fire roared cheerfully in the great fire place, and sent its sparks whirling up the chimney.

Miss Molly said: "How lovely!" and went to

stand beside it; while Joey Hub, who in all his
life had never seen such a fire, came toward it
fascinated, holding out his chapped hands grate-
fully yet without saying a word.

Miss Molly looked at the boy who was staring
at the fire, all unconscious of anything else. She
had always heard what a bad boy Joey Hub was;
quite the worst boy in the whole village everyone
said. She thought that he didn't seem such a terrible person as he stood there, his black eyes shining with delight as the big log parted suddenly,
and sent up a stream of dancing sparks. Perhaps
he wasn't so bad after all. People did exaggerate
very often, and certainly he looked like any other
small boy; not at all like the village black sheep.

She said suddenly: "Do you like it, Joey?"

He murmured something and moved away
quickly; but his eyes had spoken for him. From
then on Miss Molly made up her mind not to
believe everything she had heard about Joey
Hub.

"Miss Molly," said Mr. Hollins, coming toward her, "we are about to play 'Open-the-gate-
as-high-as-the-sky.' Will you be so good as to
hold the gates with me, ma'am?"

"Why that'll be nice," smiled Miss Molly, and
pulled off her silken gloves. "Where shall we
stand, Mr. Hollins?"

"Get in line!" sang out Milt. "Everybody get
in line for 'Open-the-gates-as-high-as-the-sky,'

and everybody get ready to pull like the dickens at the end!"

"Get in line, Joey!" Martie Martin invited him into the line beside her.

"Aw, I'll watch. I don't know how to play," Joey Hub answered.

"No fair watching," called Milt. "Everybody in line. Come on!"

"Please, Joey," Martie said, and Joey Hub took his place beside the others and the game went on toward that exciting moment when the two sides were lined up one against the other to see which was the stronger. Thanks to Joey, perhaps, the side that he was on won, and he joined in the shout of victory with the others.

Other games followed. The little O'Briens knew any number of them. They were not bashful and there wasn't a dull moment; the time, in fact, fairly flew, and everybody was deep in a new game taught them by Patsy O'Brien, when the doors to the dining room were thrown open.

There stood Mary Ann in her best white apron with the jaunty little cap to match, saying, while every tooth flashed a radiant smile, "Pigeon, honey, yo' party am served."

Her eyes caught sight of Joey Hub and widened to their full extent until only the whites were visible. Next they swept onward to the small, noisy O'Briens and it seemed for a moment that they were likely to pop right out of her head.

"How come?" she inquired in a stage whisper to Rob who was the nearest to her.

"Search me," was the answer. "Pigeon can tell you;" then he added quickly: "We're having a grand party, Mary Ann; don't you go spoil it."

"Who, me?" was the answer. "I wouldn't spoil it for anything, my baby's birthday party! Hu!" With her most ingratiating air she invited them into the dining room.

"If Mother was here," Pigeon cried, "she would play the grand march."

"I'll play for you," offered Miss Molly, and she sat down at the piano and struck a chord.

"Everybody choose a partner for the grand march! We're going into the dining room now," called Pigeon gaily.

"Oh! look! look!" The little O'Briens clasped their hands and stared with all their eyes, and indeed it was a sight well worth looking at.

In the very center of the table stood the big birthday cake with its seven candles burning brightly. On either side of it were bowls of fruit, silver bon-bon dishes filled with candies, and plates containing the delicious little cakes; and last — but in no wise least — the ice cream.

Pigeon sat at the head and Mr. Hollins sat at the foot, and when the paper caps were put on, his was in the shape of an old woman's bonnet with strings tied under the chin, and when he put it on without cracking a smile, everybody went off into shouts of laughter.

It was a merry party. The six little O'Briens managed to eat and talk as well. Micky told one joke after another, all of them very amusing; and Katie O'Brien knew nearly as many as her brother. Milt told quite a few himself and so did Rob, while Pigeon asked a riddle that even Mr. Hollins could not answer. Miss Molly remembered one she had known ever since she was a little girl, and nobody could guess that either.

When Pigeon stood up to cut the birthday cake, after Julia had handed her the big knife, everybody clapped and clapped and the four little Martins called out:

"Happy birthday, Pigeon," and gave seven cheers, one for each year, you understand. The others joined in until the great room echoed and reëchoed with the cheering.

"Speech! Speech!" cried Mr. Hollins. "Speech! Speech!" shouted the rest. "Make us a speech, do, Pigeon!"

Pigeon stood up in her little pale blue frock with the candle light on her hair and in her eyes.

"I'm so glad you came to my birthday party," she told them, "so very glad; and I do hope that you are having as good a time as I am."

"We are!" they called.

"You bet!" laughed Micky O'Brien. "We are that!"

After all the guests had gone; when the truck had been loaded with the squealing, laughing O'Briens; with Miss Molly tucked in beside them; after Mr. Hollins had mounted his wheel and Joey Hub (who had chosen to walk) had departed, the five little Martins went back into the deserted living room together with Jimmie who had remained to talk things over.

"It was a funny party," exclaimed Sarah, seating herself on the couch before the fire, "still I liked it."

"So did I," Martie agreed, nodding her bright head emphatically. "Wasn't Miss Molly sweet? She seemed to have such a good time. How'd you happen to think of inviting them, Pigeon?"

"It was Jimmie who thought of it," her sister answered. "At least Jimmie thought of Joey Hub and I thought of the O'Briens; then I thought of Miss Molly and he thought of Mr. Hollins; that was the way it was."

Rob Martin turned to his friend: "What made you think of it first off, old top?"

That young gentleman who was sunk in the depths of a big chair, while on his head there still perched the tall red paper cap, made answer, as he crossed his legs and leaned back contentedly.

"I guess it was that party in our lesson made me think of it."

"You mean," Martie turned to inquire, "about the man who made a great supper, don't you?"

Jimmie nodded. "Sure. That's it," he said.

"I'm glad Jimmie remembered 'bout it," Pigeon declared. "I'm glad I asked them, I am."

"And I'm no end glad they came," Milt agreed. "Say, I hope I can remember that joke Micky O'Brien told; it was a good one."

Outside in the twilight a little boy trudged toward the cottage which was home to him. Through his brain thoughts were flashing, one thought after the other in rapid succession.

"Gosh, what a lot to eat; all a fellow could hold." Then other thoughts came. "That fire! Such a big one, and the sparks — red as — as the berries that came from the woods at Christmas. How they flew up the big chimney; where to? They had played games. Nobody had started anything; there hadn't been a fight, not even a little one. Milt Martin, he had been nice. He wasn't a sissy; not he. He could swim further 'n any boy on the school picnic; yet he wasn't all the time starting things. Perhaps you didn't have to be a sissy not to; and Micky O'Brien — he liked Micky — he oughtn't to have thrown the dead mouse at Patsy that day maybe —"

On through the twilight, thoughts racing hither and thither, went little Joey Hub, home from the party.

His mother would be there, waiting to hear all about it. Well he had something for her, wrapped carefully in the clean handkerchief she had given him as he was leaving was the piece of birthday cake with its white and pink icing that had been given him; and beside it in his pocket was the high pointed cap.

He had much to tell her about this the very first party he had ever taken part in, had Joey Hub.

CHAPTER XIV

THE NEW TEACHER

IT was Saturday morning and Pigeon was on her way to school.

Never before in all her life had Pigeon gone to school on a Saturday morning. It gave her a queer, topsy-turvey feeling to be doing it, quite as if the days in the week had somehow become mixed. It made her feel most uncomfortable besides.

The houses she passed seemed to be asking: "Haven't you made a mistake, child? This is Saturday; one stays at home on Saturday, one does not go to school." The sun seemed to be saying that something was wrong.

"Here I am," it seemed to say. "Here I am up early and shining my best so as to give you children a glorious day out of doors; and away you go and spend it in the schoolroom. What is the meaning of it all, I'd like to know?"

The new teacher could have told. It was because of the new teacher, and by her command, that the third grade was trudging to school on this bright beautiful Saturday morning, when all the other grades were out enjoying themselves. The new teacher had been with the third grade

a whole month now. It had been the most difficult
month the third grade had ever experienced;
they were no nearer understanding each other at
the end of it than they had been at the beginning. Sometimes they looked at her and wondered why.

Miss Gray was what might be called a
'wouldn't let' person. There was her hair for instance; it wanted to curl and Miss Gray wouldn't
let it. If a single curl managed to escape, Miss
Gray soon found it out and fastened it severely
back with a hair pin. There was Miss Gray's
mouth; it was a mouth intended for smiles, but
did Miss Gray allow it to? Oh, dear, no! She kept
it in a firm, red line so that not a single smile
could find its way through. There were Miss
Gray's eyes, lovely blue ones, which were intended to dance and shine and sparkle, only Miss
Gray wouldn't let them. Oh, dear, no! There was
Miss Gray's voice; surely it was a voice intended to say pleasant things, kind, helpful
things, to small, eager third graders, only Miss
Gray wouldn't let it. Oh dear, no! Instead she
made it say hard, uncomfortable things, things
that made little children squirm and feel angry
and hurt; things like, "Take two demerits and
remain after school is over."

From the very first day the new teacher had
expected things to go wrong. They did. Each day
they seemed to go more and more so, for, as

every one knows, the surest way to make things go wrong is to expect them to. They seldom, if ever disappoint you if you do. Miss Gray expected things to go wrong, and she was not disappointed. Nothing the third grade did was right.

They could not march to suit her; they could not sit to suit her; they could not sing, nor recite, nor do a single thing to suit her. And so, after awhile, they stopped trying to please her, and from then on things went from bad to worse, until now here they were going to school on a Saturday morning with all the other grades on hand to see them go by.

The rest of the school must have breakfasted early that particular morning so as not to miss anything. As Myrtle Jones and Pigeon passed the Bell house little Dickie Bell, who was seated on the fence, began to yell at the top of his voice:

"Sat'day's scholar, not worth a dollar! a dollar! a dollar! Not worth a dollar!"

He kept it up as long as they were in sight, and they could still hear him after they had turned the corner.

"I wish, I *do* wish he'd fall off." Myrtle's face was very red. "For a crooked penny, Pigeon, I'd go right back and push him off so he'd bump his head, the horrid little thing."

"No, don't." Pigeon put out a hand to stop her. "It wouldn't do the least good, Myrtle, and besides his mother might come out and say things.

After all, we are Saturday scholars and maybe we aren't worth a dollar. At any rate Miss Gray doesn't seem to think we are."

There were tears of mortification and anger in Myrtle's eyes. "That old Miss Gray," she cried. " I — I just *can't* like her, Pigeon, I can't! "

Pigeon said thoughtfully: "Well I don't love her any too much, Myrtle; but we mustn't hate her, 'cause, you know, she is our enemy and the Bible says, plain as anything, ' Love your enemies.' "

Myrtle tossed her head. " Well, I can't love her, even if she is my enemy. I just can't, Pigeon Martin, so there! Why if it hadn't been for her I'd have been on my way this very minute to spend the day with my grandmother 'stead of, — 'stead of, — I know *one* thing; our dear, darling Miss Henderson never would have taken our Saturday away from us like this, never! "

" Please don't let's talk about Miss Henderson right now," Pigeon exclaimed. " 'Cause even just thinkin' 'bout her makes me feel awful queer way down deep in my stomach. Myrtle, I wish you hadn't said it. I wish you hadn't gone and mentioned Miss Henderson's name. I feel — I feel I'm going to cry! "

Myrtle caught hold of her arm.

" Don't you dare, Pigeon. If you do all those girls and boys over there'll think it's 'cause you have to go back to school. Goodness knows, it's bad enough to have to go back, but to have 'em think you're cryin' 'bout it! Oh, Pigeon, you mustn't! Listen, Pigeon, listen to me. We've got to be laughin' when we go by, laughin' like anything. We just must!"

The smaller girl nodded and gulped, swallowed hard, threw up her little brown head and began to swing the strap which held her books with a jaunty air of unconcern.

"All right, Myrtle, I'm ready. Let's begin to laugh."

The worst thing that had happened had occurred yesterday. It was just after recess, that period when the third grade were supposed to be busy with their number work; only some of them it seems, were not. Bobby Mason, for example, was engaged in drawing pictures on his tablet. First Bobby had drawn a horse, then a dog, then something intended for an airplane, but which resembled a kite far more. Presently he had taken a clean sheet of paper and gone to work upon another picture, bending over his desk and not letting anyone see it until it was finished. Once finished, Bobby held it up, ready to slip it into his desk at a moment's notice, so that everyone could take a look at what he had drawn.

Now Bobby was not much of an artist; still everyone knew whose likeness the drawing was intended for. Besides, if there had been the slightest doubt about it, Bobby made it plain, for there, coming out of the mouth of the lady, was a big, round " Don't!"

Miss Gray, who was at the blackboard at that moment explaining an example, and had her back to the room, said suddenly in a most dreadful voice:

" Robert Mason, bring me that paper!"

Bobby said afterwards that she must have eyes in the back of her head, or how else could she have known that he had a paper?

A little gasp went round the room, everyone turned and looked at Bobby, who had gone a most remarkable red, even to the roots of his hair, while his eyes had grown big and frightened. What would Miss Gray do to him? What would she not do?

He got up slowly, just as if his feet wouldn't work properly. They did seem heavy and quite reluctant to carry him at all; and, when at last they did, they went dragging across the room, one after another, carrying him to where Miss Gray waited, so cold and stern and angry. Poor Bobby!

Miss Gray reached over and took the piece of tablet paper from his trembling hand. After a moment — it seemed more like days and hours to the waiting third grade — she spoke.

" And so," she said, " and so, Master Robert Mason, this is my picture, is it? This is intended for a likeness of me."

" Aw, Miss Gray," began Bobby, squirming uncomfortably and unable to lift his eyes from the floor. " Aw, Miss Gray, I didn't mean — "

. " That will do," she interrupted. " I understand. I understand perfectly. This is what you think of your teacher. This is what you all think, is it? Very well. Now I will tell you just what your teacher thinks of you."

Then and there she had started in to tell the third grade what she thought of them, and there wasn't a single nice thing about it. They were the most exasperating children it had ever fallen to her lot to teach; the most disagreeable, the most trying, the most unruly; and to punish them in the way that they deserved to be punished, she intended to take away their holiday and make them come back to school on Saturday. That might, perhaps, in time, teach them to behave like civilized beings and not like a pack of little Hottentots. As for Bobby Mason, she would have more to say to him after school was over. Later they had marched out and left Bobby standing in the corner looking very miserable, and none of them would have liked to be in Bobby's shoes.

" Hey, Pigeon, wait! "

They were passing the door of Sallie Bell French's house when she came running out. Her eyes were sparkling, her face was flushed; it was plain to see she was excited over something. Quite a number of other children had by now joined Myrtle and Pigeon and it was from these that she drew Pigeon aside.

"Cross-your-heart-and-hope-you-may-die-if-you-tell, and I'll tell you a secret," she whispered in Pigeon's ear.

Obediently Pigeon did as she was told. "You'll have to hurry and tell me, Sallie Bell," she said. "The others are leaving me behind."

Sallie Bell said: "Listen, Pigeon, listen to me. There won't be any school today after all!"

Pigeon stared.

"Why not? Why won't there?"

Sallie Bell giggled and tossed her head. She looked most important as she told the round-eyed Pigeon: "It's the very biggest kind of a secret; only three people know it, Ken Burton, John Smith and I (only they don't know I know). You've promised not to tell; don't forget, Pigeon. You'd get me into terrible trouble if you did."

"I'll not tell, of course, Sallie Bell," Pigeon promised. "Only do hurry. I don't dare be late; there's no telling what Miss Gray would do to me if I were."

"But I tell you, Pigeon," Sallie Bell exclaimed, "there isn't going to be any school today; there can't be because of that dreadful smell."

"What dreadful smell? What are you talking about? Aren't you coming to school yourself, Sallie Bell?"

Sallie Bell shook her head. "I've got to go

to the dentist. Mother's going to send Miss Gray a note tellin' her. I had tooth-ache all night, Pigeon; it's only a little better now and — "

"Oh, but the secret, Sallie Bell," Pigeon interrupted. "'Course I'm dreadful sorry 'bout your tooth, and now I've got to run to catch up with the others. Goodbye."

"Listen, Pigeon. Mary Burton came home from school yesterday and she was cryin' 'cause of the things Miss Gray said to us. It made Ken mad as anything 'cause he's dreadful fond of his little sister Mary; so he told her not to cry and he'd promise to fix things so there wouldn't be any school or anything. Of course he didn't tell Mary what it was he was going to do."

"Well, what was he going to do?" Pigeon asked in some impatience. Sallie Bell had such a long way of going all around Robin Hood's barn, especially when she was excited, and she was excited now. She kept twisting her handkerchief into a little ball and untwisting it again all the time she was talking.

"Don't hurry a person so, Pigeon. I'm coming to that as fast as I can. I don't believe you appreciate my telling you the secret anyway; you don't act as if you did."

"You haven't told it to me, and besides I've got to go."

"Wait a minute." Sallie Bell put out a hand to

hold her back. "You are the very most impatient person, Pigeon Martin, the very most impatient person in the whole world, so there! I don't believe I'll tell you my secret. Yes, I will too. Listen, what do you s'pose those boys, Ken and John Smith, went and did? They got some perfectly horrid smelling stuff from the drug store and they sprinkled it all over the third grade room, desks and everything; so nobody can stay in it long at a time."

"Oh," cried Pigeon. "How'd you know, Sallie Bell?"

"It was this way," Sallie Bell, who was enjoying herself immensely, went on to explain. "I was in the hen house this morning looking for eggs. Mother gives me two pennies for every egg I find. Well, I heard someone coming through our yard, so I looked through a crack in the door, and I saw Ken and John. They were laughing like anything and Ken said it would serve the old cat right for being so mean to us kids, and then he said; 'Did you put a lot round her desk, John?' And John answered; 'You bet I did.' Ken said he'd used up a whole bottle of iodoform but if he had another bottle he'd go back and put that one too. Now you know the secret, Pigeon, you are the only person I've breathed it to. My, those boys would be mad as hops if they knew I knew. Cross your heart again, Pigeon, you won't tell!"

"I won't. I promise I won't," Pigeon answered as she set off on a run to overtake the others.

Myrtle was looking a trifle cross as she came up.

"That Sallie Bell French makes me tired," she exclaimed. "Always whisperin' 'bout something. Who wants to know her old secret anyway? I'm sure I don't." She gave her head a toss. "I wouldn't even listen if she tried to tell me. Was it a nice secret, Pigeon?"

Pigeon shook her head.

"No, Myrtle, it wasn't," she said.

They were nearing the school house.

How big and solemn it looked today with all its many windows, like great eyes peering down at them as if to inquire what they were doing there? The big door was wide open, like a vast mouth waiting to swallow them up, and it seemed to say:

"Come right along in, you bad little third graders, having to come back on a Saturday morning. I'm surprised at you, I am indeed."

In they went.

Down the long hall, which echoed with the sound of their footsteps, past closed doors on either side, on and on toward their own room at the far end of the hall, where Miss Gray was waiting for them. Miss Gray, who had called them a pack of little Hottentots, whose eyes were angry and hurt and cold and unloving.

As they neared the door a strange odor came floating out to them. A most disagreeable odor indeed.

They put their handkerchiefs to their noses and sniffed. It was so strong, so penetrating. It filled their throats and eyes; there seemed to be no getting away from it, it was everywhere. Even though the windows and doors were wide open, the smell seemed to fill the entire room, to hang from the walls, to rise from the floor. It was, as Sallie Bell had said, dreadful.

And there in the midst of it stood the new teacher, standing beside her desk as they filed silently in.

Her head was high, her lips were set in a straighter, redder line than ever before, while her face was a sort of sickly gray. There was a queer look in her eyes; worse than yesterday, when they had been angry.

The third grade took their places without a word, they had a feeling that something that they had never experienced before was about to happen. They felt awed and still and decidedly queer.

Once Jimmie Adkins opened his mouth to ask a question. He took one look at his teacher and the question went unasked. Jimmie decided hastily that this was no time in which to seek information, no time at all.

The rest of the third grade must have felt the same way about it, for no questions were asked

this morning; instead they sat, with their handkerchiefs to their noses, and waited.

Miss Gray let them wait. She let them wait
quite awhile, she seemed in no great hurry to begin, but stood there moving the pens and pencils
about on her desk and biting her lips, and the
hand that touched the pencils trembled. The
third grade, sitting for all the world like a parcel
of little wooden children, stared at her. It was
just as though they were playing some sort of
silly game. After a long time Miss Gray spoke.

If what she said to them yesterday had been
unkind, what she said to them today was enough
to make them weep. When she had finished some
of them were crying. Some of the girls had their
heads down upon the desk while some of the boys
looked as though they would have liked to do the
same if they hadn't been boys. All of them were
looking as solemn as owls in a tree, while all
about them there was stillness and the smell.

"And now," said Miss Gray sternly, " Now
comes this last outrageous piece of mischief, this
unpardonable performance — I can find no words
in which to tell you just what I think of it."

She paused as if unable to go on, while her
eyes, still with that queer expression in them as if
she had not slept at all, traveled from one face
to the other.

" I have no idea which of you is responsible for
this," she said. " But I mean to know and to

know at once. I shall give you a chance to confess of your own accord; and I tell you frankly that, if you do not, it will go badly with you."

One of the girls sobbed aloud at this. Pigeon was not among those crying, as she did not feel in the least like crying. She felt that Miss Gray was being unfair and unjust. She had jumped immediately to the conclusion that someone in the third grade had put the iodoform about the schoolroom, and she believed it as truly as she did that she was standing at her desk.

"Well," she said, and her voice was like ice. "Well, I'm waiting."

There was a long, long moment when if anyone had dropped a pin it would have sounded the length of the room, so still was everything. Even the weeping ones seemed to hold their breath for what was to come next.

It came.

Miss Gray took a step forward, her face suddenly crimson.

"I see," she said. "I see that none of you mean to own up, therefore I shall begin and ask each of you in turn, and I trust that you will see fit to tell me the truth about it."

Pigeon drew herself up proudly, her small head high. The idea, the very idea of supposing for a moment that any one of the third grade would lie to get themselves out of a piece of mischief. She rather guessed not. For a moment the little girl felt herself wishing that some member of the third grade had done this thing, since Miss Gray was so certain that they had.

"Nancy Ellis," began their teacher. "Did you put this iodoform in the schoolroom? If not, do you know who did?"

Nancy was one of the weeping ones so instead of answering she only wept the louder and, after a little, Miss Gray was forced to accept Nancy's tears as a sign that she had neither put it there nor knew who had, and go on to the next.

"Jimmie Adkins," asked Miss Gray, in a voice of steel. "Do you or do you not know anything about this?"

"I do not."

Jimmie answered so loud that everybody jumped. Bobby Mason sat next to Jimmie. Bobby felt certain that Miss Gray thought him the guilty party because of what had happened the day before. He did look as though he might have been, for his face was as red as it had been when he had walked up to give his teacher the picture he had drawn. Everybody was looking straight at him, and all were wondering if perhaps he had not done this thing to get even with Miss Gray. As for Miss Gray she was looking sterner than ever as she said:

"What do you know about this, Robert Mason?"

Bobby managed to stumble to his feet and to answer earnestly, looking her right in the eyes: "I don't know a single thing about it; honest, Miss Gray, I don't."

Even Miss Gray couldn't help believing what he said in spite of his red face, his grey eyes were so clear, so honest. Her lips tightened quickly, and she looked most severely at Bobby; but she went right on to the next, asking of each in turn: "Did you put the iodoform in the room? If you did not, do you know who did?"

With each, "No, Miss Gray," she seemed to grow more vexed until Pigeon watching her wished devoutly that Sallie Bell had kept her old secret to herself. Nearer and nearer Miss Gray was approaching her row, and now she had begun upon it. In the second seat from the front she sat and waited; her hands clasped themselves in her lap, her breath came fast, and from a long distance she seemed to hear her teacher's voice asking:

"Mary Frances Martin, do you know anything about this?"

Poor, little unhappy Pigeon felt her face go as red as Bobby's had been. She felt the room begin to whirl about her, and heard her voice, very faint, very far away, saying in answer:

"Yes, Miss Gray, I do; but oh, please, Miss Gray, it wasn't anyone in the third grade; really it wasn't."

An astonished gasp went around the room, and even Miss Gray looked surprised. For a moment she did not speak. One of those dreadful moments of silence followed, the kind that is hardest to break, while every eye in the room was fixed on Pigeon; round eyes, amazed eyes filled with questions.

"Tell me at once," commanded that stern voice; "who put the iodoform in the room."

Little Mary Frances Martin braced her feet against the iron holders that fastened her desk to the floor; for about her the room was still whirling, and the floor seemed to fly up and hit her — bang — in the face. She replied quaveringly:

"I — I can't tell you, Miss Gray, because I promised not to."

Again a gasp ran around the room. Miss Gray took a step toward her, uttering just two words, but those two were like a pistol shot in the stillness.

"You must!" she said.

There was silence while the big, round clock on the schoolroom wall ticked away the seconds.

"Did you hear, Mary Frances? I am waiting for you to answer me."

"Poor, miserable child!" the round clock seemed to say. "Poor you! I'm glad I'm not in your shoes!"

Miss Gray spoke. "A bad promise," she said, "is better broken than kept. Answer my question,

Mary Frances, was it you who put this in the school? "

"Oh, no, indeed," said Pigeon quickly. " I never thought of such a thing!"

" Then you do know who put it there? "

Pigeon remembered her promise. "Yes, Miss Gray, I do. But I can't tell; I promised not to."

" Poor Mary Frances! Poor you! " ticked the round-faced clock on the wall. " I'm sorry for you, I'm sorry for you! Sorry, sorry! "

Pigeon was sorry for herself.

Miss Gray turned to the others. " You are dismissed," she told them. " You may go, now, at once, all except Mary Frances Martin. She will remain until after she has answered my question. One — two — three."

Pigeon watched them turn, rise and march out of the room, leaving her to her fate. She caught the look of silent sympathy in Myrtle's eyes, heard Jimmie Adkins' quick whisper, as he passed her desk, " Good for you! Pigeon Martin, don't you let her make you tell," and then she was all alone with Miss Gray — Miss Gray and that horrid sickening smell and the round-faced clock upon the wall.

" Come with me," said the new teacher. " It's quite impossible to stay longer in here."

She held open the door and they marched, like a jailer with a prisoner the child thought, down the long, empty corridor and on to the first grade room where Miss Gray opened the door and pointed to one of the many empty seats. She seated herself wearily at the teacher's desk and looked at Pigeon.

It was a relief to be away from the smell; a relief to be able to breathe without having one's lungs filled with it, without feeling it up one's nose and making one's eyes water. The first grade room was a most cheerful place. About its walls were brightly colored pictures of animals and children; in all of its big windows geraniums bloomed gaily. Upon the blackboard there was the picture of a hen crayoned red, and underneath, in white letters, was printed, so that the first grade might read, " See the red hen."

Looking at it Pigeon thought of Chuckle, Sarah's fat, speckled hen, and thinking of Chuckle made her wonder just what was happening at home at the present moment. Were they all down by the Elegant Tree? Perhaps they were skating on the pond, doing curves on the ice. It was frozen over now, smooth and clear like a great looking-glass. Oh, dear, there was always so much to do on a Saturday at the Martin House, so many delightful things; and here she was shut up in a schoolroom with nothing to do but look at the picture of a red hen.

" Well," asked Miss Gray, " are you still stubborn, or have you made up your mind to answer my question? "

" Please, Miss Gray," Pigeon's voice sounded

very faint and small. " I'm not being stubborn. I just can't tell; I promised not to."

" You mean that you won't. Very well, then, we shall stay here until you do, remember that."

They sat on. It seemed to Pigeon that it was centuries and centuries that they sat there. She began to wish Miss Gray would say something; anything was better than just sitting there in silence. She twisted uncomfortably in the very little seat and sighed a great, big sigh. She wondered if Miss Gray intended to keep her there all night as well as all day? What would they think at home when the stars began to come out, when the others came in from play, and there was no Mary Frances? Would they form a searching party and go out to scour the country for a little lost girl? If they did would they ever think of coming to school to look for her, or would they just suppose she had been stolen on her way home and never think of going near the schoolhouse? She felt certain that she could not stay awake all the night through, and equally certain that Miss Gray would never allow her to sleep, not even to take one little nap. She felt that she would be obliged to sit up straight hour after hour the long night through.

" Mary Frances Martin," the voice of the teacher interrupted her reveries. " I have waited long enough. Answer my question at once; tell me who put the iodoform about the schoolroom! "

" I can't tell you, Miss Gray."

CHAPTER XV

The Picnic

THERE was silence in the room. Utter silence, broken only by the tap, tap, of the teacher's pencil upon the desk. The big cheerful room with its red geraniums, its gay colored balls for counting, its bright pictures, the red hen on the blackboard, all seemed to become dark and dreary as a frightened child faced her teacher and refused to do as she had been bidden.

" Are you going to tell me, Mary Frances? "

" No, Miss Gray."

" Very well then; listen to me. I mean what I say. Here you will stay until you do."

They sat on. Thoughts crowded themselves into little Mary Frances' sleek, brown head; long thoughts, queer thoughts. Her foot went to sleep and she dared not stand up or try to walk to waken it. Her whole body was cramped and weary from sitting still so long, especially in such a small chair. She yawned and sighed again; she was sure now that it must be near lunch time. Oh, dear, how tired she was! What a long morning! Well, she didn't need to starve anyway. Mother had given her two sandwiches that morning, two luscious sandwiches wrapped in oiled paper; why not have a bite of one now? Miss Gray was not looking at her; instead she had her eyes shut. Perhaps she was asleep. This was a good time to take out the sandwiches which were in the pocket of her dress. Carefully she drew them out. A hurried glance in the teacher's direction showed that she had not moved or opened her eyes; now was the time!

Pigeon hastily slipped off the paper and took a bite. Did anything ever taste so good before? She thought not. One more hurried bite and then she paused, staring in amazement. She could not believe her eyes. There, there upon Miss Gray's cheek was a tear; and even as she gazed another stole silently from under her closed lids. Miss Gray and tears! Was anything harder to believe?

And strange as it may seem, Pigeon found herself feeling sorry for Miss Gray. She began to remember many things, things that weren't so pleasant for Miss Gray. She remembered that her teacher had to get up early with only a boarding-house breakfast to begin the day with. She pictured her hurrying off to school, to be met with that dreadful odor everywhere, and thinking that it had been put there just to hurt her, to show her how much her pupils disliked her. The more Pigeon thought the sorrier she felt; then, without knowing how she got there, she found herself standing by the teacher's desk holding out the other sandwich and saying eagerly:

"Please, Miss Gray, take it, won't you? Mother made it and it's good."

At the words, Miss Gray lifted her head and gazed, first at Pigeon and then at the sandwich held out to her. Then, to the child's utter consternation, down went her teacher's head upon the desk, and she wept as though her heart would break.

"Miss Gray! Oh, please don't, Miss Gray! Don't feel so badly. Please take my sandwich; and oh, Miss Gray, please, please, believe that none of the third grade put that dreadful stuff about."

Presently Miss Gray took out her handkerchief and wiped her eyes; then she tried to smile, and her voice wasn't like ice any longer; it was gentle and kind and she was letting it be. "Mary Frances," she said, "tell me, won't you, why is it that the third grade dislike me so?"

And straight off came the answer. "It's because you don't like us, Miss Gray."

For a moment Miss Gray did not reply. She seemed to be turning the answer over in her mind. Then she nodded. "There's a good deal in that," she said. And then to the little girl's amazement she put an arm about her and drew her close: "Do you think," she asked, "that I can ever make the third grade like me?"

Pigeon answered earnestly. "If you tried, you could make them love you, Miss Gray."

Her teacher smiled, although there were still tears in her eyes. Then quite unexpectedly she laughed. Pigeon started, for it was the first time that she had ever heard her teacher laugh. She hadn't ever really supposed that she could, and here she was with the very sweetest, merriest laugh imaginable. It was the kind that made you want to laugh with her; the kind that began with her eyes and ended with her lips. Think of possessing a laugh like that and never using it; never letting thirty little children know that you had it even!

Miss Gray stopped laughing and looked at Pigeon. "You are thinking," she asked, "what?"

"I was thinking," answered the child, "that I didn't know you could laugh like that."

Miss Gray answered thoughtfully, as she reached out to take the sandwich:

"My, what a mistake I've made! What a lot I'll have to undo. Will you help me, little Mary Frances, child?"

Looking at her Pigeon answered: "If you'd only let them hear you laugh like that, they just couldn't help loving you, Miss Gray."

Miss Gray laughed again, then she said quite soberly: "There's something I want to say to you, dear, and that is that I'm sorry, very sorry, that I tried to make you tell me when you had promised not to. Will you forgive me and let us start all over again? "

Then before Pigeon could answer there was a knock on the door, and in answer to Miss Gray's "Come in," it opened and her brother Milton stood there.

"Say, I've been looking for you everywhere, Pigeon," he said. "What on earth are you doing in here?" His eyes widened as he saw Miss Gray with an arm about his sister.

As Mary Frances looked at Milton standing there in his old white sweater with the collar rolled about his uncovered head, all rumpled and wind blown; his eyes so bright and his cheeks and lips as red as apples in winter, she thought of what Bettina had said the other night when he had come into the living-room with an armful of wood for the fire. "Doesn't Milt look like the Spirit of Winter," she had exclaimed, and Mary Frances remembered it now as he stood there saying to Miss Gray:

"Please, Miss Gray, our uncle has a big sleigh and we are going for a picnic in the woods. I've come to ask if you won't let Mary Frances go with us? We all think it wouldn't be exactly a picnic if Mary Frances was left behind; so please, Miss Gray, say that she may come along."

"Why of course," Miss Gray answered smiling. "Of course she may go. I quite agree with you that a picnic wouldn't be a picnic at all unless

it included Mary Frances. A picnic in the winter
time; what a charming idea! How perfectly
scrumptious!" (Yes she did, she said just exactly
those words!)

The moment she spoke you could see Milt
thinking. It was plain that he was making up his
mind about something. First he opened his eyes
as wide as he could, then he screwed them up
tightly. He gave the new teacher of grade three
a long, long look. Perhaps he caught some of
the wistfulness in her dark eyes, which seemed
to be saying as plain as anything: "Please,
please like me, Mary Frances' brother, please
do. I can be gay and young and jolly. Try me
and see."

"Say, Miss Gray," cried the boy, taking a step
forward, "won't you come to the picnic with us?"

"Oh!" Pigeon could scarcely believe her ears.
"Please do," she said. As for Miss Gray, she
glanced from one to the other. Her cheeks were
a sudden pink and her eyes sparkled. "Do—do
you mean it?" she asked.

"You bet we do," Milt answered laughing;
and Pigeon cried, "Oh, I know where we are
going; it's just the very loveliest place in which
to have a picnic. Please, Miss Gray, won't you
come?"

"Yes, come along, Miss Gray."

The Spirit of Winter stood there smiling, inviting her out into the sunshine, out to where the

snow lay deep under the pines, out into the glorious day beyond the schoolroom and the troubles of the morning. " Please do," he begged.

Miss Gray rose from her seat. "You are sure," she asked, "that my coming wouldn't spoil the party? You really and truly want me to come?"

" Try us and see," answered the boy.

" And you, little Mary Frances, do you want me on your picnic, dear?"

And strange as it may seem, never in all her life had Pigeon wanted anything so much as she wanted Miss Gray to come to the picnic. " Oh, yes, yes, Miss Gray," she answered earnestly, " I do want you; I do. Please come."

" Very well," smiled her teacher. " Then I will."

" Good!" Milt exclaimed. "We'll have to hurry. I lost a lot of time looking for Pigeon. We are going to meet the others at the cross-roads. I say, what's that awful thing I smell?"

Milton was wrinkling his nose and sniffing. On her way to the hall to fetch her hat Miss Gray called back over her shoulder: " Oh, dear, isn't it horrid? Somebody thought it would be funny to sprinkle iodoform around the third grade room so as to annoy me. It wasn't anyone in the third grade, however, so it really doesn't matter at all."

Pigeon's eyes flew wide open. Had she heard aright? Could this be the same Miss Gray who had so recently marched her through the hall like a prisoner? The same Miss Gray who had spoken so sternly; who had bidden her stay in school until she answered her question? Could this Miss Gray who was coming toward her with a little blue hat pulled over her hair and a blue coat with a fur collar, be the same severe person of the morning? Surely not; for this Miss Gray was smiling, there was a little curl which bobbed delightfully about her forehead, and her eyes were gay and kind and friendly. She had ceased to be a 'wouldn't-let' person altogether.

"Ready?" she laughed. "Let's go!"

"Let's go!" answered Milt. "Maybe we'll have to run so as not to keep 'em waiting."

"Certainly," was the answer. "Let's run by all means." And before Milt could say anything she was off and away through the gates and on down the hill, running as fast and as easily as the boy by her side. Pigeon, following behind, heard the sound of sleigh bells in the distance. How good it was to be out in the sunshine of that winter's day! Oh, how very good! She drew in great breaths of the fresh, sparkling air and felt her spirits rising with every step.

They were waiting for her at the foot of the hill. Miss Gray's hat had slipped off, and she was carrying it in her hand, while about her face her dark hair was curling in soft little waves of silk. Milt was telling her something and they were both laughing as the little girl came up.

Here they come. Sleigh bells growing louder. Laughing voices joining with them. Uncle Bob on the driver's seat, and Father beside him; the others tucked in at the back under heavy robes and cushions. Everybody waving, calling out a greeting, the sunshine on the horses' backs making them glisten like satin; the crack of the long whip in the air; a picnic in winter. Joy! Fun!

"Hey, Pigeon! Hey, Milt! How do you do, Miss Gray?"

"Whoa there! whoa! Tumble in everybody!"

"Here, Pigeon, sit by me."

"No, she's going to sit here."

"Give me your hand, Miss Gray; let me help you up. So glad you are coming with us."

"Here, Milt old man, scramble up somewhere. Whoa there! whoa!"

"Sit here, Miss Gray. Don't you think we are brave to attempt a picnic with snow on the ground?"

"I think it's just the loveliest idea; it's so dear in the children to ask me."

"We're glad you came. I'm glad of a chance to really know Mary Frances' teacher. There's nothing like a picnic for getting really acquainted, is there?"

"Well, Bob, we are all in, let's be off."

"Get up!"

"No, wait, wait a minute. Sarah has dropped her hat."

" I'll get it."

" Sit still, Rob is after it."

Under cover of the noise Bettina whispered to Pigeon: " You never told me she was pretty." And Pigeon whispered back: " I never knew it until just a little while ago."

Sarah and Martie were both making round eyes at her, eyes which said as plain as words: " However did it happen? "

Sarah tugged at her sleeve. " Tell me," she began. " Hush," whispered Pigeon, " I'll tell you all about it when we get there."

Bells jingling, — sunshine, — laughter, — snow upon the hillside, — pines tall, stately, green, — the road a grey ribbon leading on and on, — there in the heart of the grove a sheltered spot, — all out. The picnic had begun.

" Pigeon, I can't wait another moment. I say, Pigeon, she's as nice as nice, and you said — "

" Yes, Sarah, but I didn't know then. I just found it out."

" I nearly fell out of the sleigh when I saw who it was with you and Milt."

" I guess you did. I'm surprised myself. Come over here and I'll tell you all about it. Look at Miss Gray and Bettina walking with their arms about one another's waists just as if they'd known one another always."

" They've found out that they belong to the same sorority," explained Martie. " Their tongues are going lickity-split as fast as anything. I wish I was old enough to go away to college; it must be heaps of fun."

"Yes, but you'd have to leave Mother and Father and everything to go, you know."

"Yes, of course, I never thought of that. Miss Gray is awfully pretty, isn't she? You must have exaggerated when you said she was cross."

Their mother called: "Come, lazy folks, and help set the table. Martie, you and Sarah gather some pine cones to hold down the ends of the table cloth; and Mary Frances, you may bring the cups from the basket. Hurry, dear."

A picnic in the winter time! The sunshine sparkling down upon a white cloth, fastened at each end by a big pine cone, on the brown and white of chicken, the red of ham, the yellow of butter, the green of salad, the white and gold of eggs. Father bending over the fire to turn the potatoes in the coals, bacon sizzling; coffee for the grown-ups, chocolate and milk for the young folks; sandwiches, plates of them; crackers, buns; was there ever such a picnic? Such appetites!

"Come along, everybody. Lunch is ready."

Father asking a blessing, while the pines murmured softly over his bent head; the fire snapping and sending up red sparks toward the blue sky; Uncle Bob cracking jokes; Mother remembering funny things they did when she was a girl!;

everybody laughing, everybody happy. Such a picnic!

"Mrs. Martin, I had forgotten that coffee could taste so delicious."

"Well, my dear, you must come to the Martin House and have it with us often."

"May I? I'd love to."

"Then see that you do. Rob, son, you'll make yourself ill; how many eggs have you eaten? "

"Only five; honest, Mother."

"Only five! Hear the boy! I'll expect him to cackle next! Here's the salt, don't eat so fast. I'll take an egg myself, if Robby's left one."

"My favorite kind of cake — mine too. Say, whoever thought up this picnic anyway? "

Later, packing the big hamper, the boys high in one of the tall trees called down to them:

"Miss Gray, toss me up a cake, won't you? Gee! We can see all over the world from here! "

It was time to be leaving. Uncle Bob was hitching the horses; the sun was sinking to sleep among the pines, while a quick little breeze sprang up suddenly. "Ough! how good the robe feels! " The horses eager to be off — all in!

The picnic was over.

CHAPTER XVI

THINGS HAPPEN

IT was the last week of school, and Pigeon was climbing Round Hill at ten minutes to nine in the morning. The loveliest flowers grew on Round Hill and the little girl thought that if she hurried she might take a bunch of them to Miss Gray.

The third grade were in love with their teacher. For months now they had known a very different Miss Gray—one who was a friend as well as a teacher. Round Hill was steep, though not very high, and not far from the schoolhouse. At the foot of it there ran a very muddy creek.

All about the creek there grew the loveliest white violets—these Pigeon especially wanted, for Miss Gray liked them best of all flowers. She was stooping over, picking as fast as she could, when one foot slipped, and before she knew it, down she went into the muddy creek, shoes, new socks, clean dress and all.

Just then the school bell rang out across the valley— and there she was.

"Come! Come! Come!" called the bell.

"Ha-ha-ha!" jeered the creek. "Much you look like going!"

Then with a mighty effort, she managed to draw forth first one foot and then the other. She scrambled up on the bank, and threw herself face downward and proceeded to howl with all her might.

"Oh, I say, is it as bad as that, really?"

Glancing up, Pigeon saw that a strange young man was standing there beside her, and looking down from behind horn-rimmed glasses.

"It's all in a day, you know," he told her.

"And besides, it might have been worse!"

"It couldn't have been worse than it is," was the indignant answer as she struggled to her knees. "These are my best shoes; this dress is almost new and the socks are quite new. 'Sides I'm late for school and you—you stand there saying things might be worse!"

"Listen, little girl." The stranger sat down on the grass beside her. "Crying never did any good; and in spite of what you think, things might have been far worse. You might have fallen all the way into the creek instead of just part way."

Pigeon was not to be comforted. "A lot of good that does. And look at my flowers. I can't take 'em to school. I was gathering them for my teacher." She choked and rubbed her eyes leaving long black streaks across her cheeks.

"For the love of Mike!" the stranger exclaimed. "Don't do that!" Hastily he reached in his pocket, wet his handkerchief in the creek and handed it to Pigeon.

"Well," he told her, "if that's the case, your teacher shouldn't be very hard on you for being late."

"Oh, she won't be hard," Pigeon said. "She used to be hard as nails but she isn't any more. But I did want her to have the violets. Miss Gray dearly loves violets."

The strange young man was staring at her.

"What's your teacher's name? Say it again, won't you; and say it very distinctly so that there won't be room for any mistake, please."

Wondering if he had suddenly lost his mind, Pigeon repeated obediently: "Miss Gray is my teacher. She likes white violets. I picked them for her."

"Wait!" He leaned toward her breathlessly, his eyes searching hers earnestly, "do you know her full name?" he demanded.

"Her name is Helen March Gray," Pigeon replied. "She teaches the third grade, and we are all just crazy about her."

"I'll bet you are!", the young man exclaimed. "So am I."

Pigeon's eyes flew wide open.

"You are wild about our Miss Gray?" she asked in amazement.

"Well," he laughed, "she happens to be my Miss Gray as well; or at least I think she is. It's this way," he went on. "Long ago, before she was your teacher; before she thought of being anybody's teacher, she and I lived on the same street and every Friday afternoon we went to the same dancing school. Now isn't this a queer old world?"

"Please," Pigeon begged, "tell me some more about the dancing shool. Were you all dressed up, you and Miss Gray with shiny slippers and all?"

"You bet we were!" He laughed "I can remember the white turn-over collar I had to wear to this day!"

"I bet you looked nice," Pigeon told him. "What did Miss Gray wear to dancing school?"

"Well," he shut his eyes for a moment. "She wore a white dress with a pink sash. She had long brown curls that came below her shoulders. I may be wrong about the sash, but I'm certain about those curls. I'll tell you something," his white teeth flashed in a smile, "I have one of those curls now, for a fact. I cut it off years ago at dancing school and she never knew the difference."

"You never told her, nev-er?"

"Nev-er. Promise me you won't either."

"Oh, course not. I wouldn't for anything. Why didn't you ever tell her?"

He looked across the valley, and he smiled. "Even then," he said, "little as she was, I was a little afraid of her. I didn't want her to be angry and I didn't want to give the curl back. She was that kind even then."

"Aren't you ever going to tell her?"

"Some day, I hope to show it to her."

"Did you come to Brentville just to see Miss Gray?"

He glanced up and answered quietly, "I came hoping I might see her."

"Oh, as to that," she told him in a matter-of-fact tone, "you won't have the slightest trouble. She boards with Miss Sallie Foster. It's the most dismalest house in the village. You can't miss it. Anybody can show you where it is."

He asked suddenly: "What's your name, little girl?"

"Mary Frances Martin," she said, "Though my family 'cept Mother, call me Pigeon. Silly, isn't it?"

"Well now, I don't know about that." he smiled, "When I was little they called me Dickie; some people do to this day. My name is Richard Cameron. My Dad and I live all alone in a big red brick house in Boston."

Pigeon wanted to know: "Did Miss Gray have a nick-name when she was little, when you went to dancing school together?"

"She did," he laughed. "We used to call her

Taffy, because of her curls. In the sun they were the color of taffy candy, but they are darker now. Little Mary Frances," he asked, "are you the kind who can keep a secret?"

Pigeon nodded; "I never tell a secret; wild horses couldn't make me. Myrtle and I have a perfectly splendid one. Martie and Sarah have been trying to make me tell, but I wouldn't— not for anything. Is your secret about Miss Gray?"

"Yes," he answered. "It is. You see it isn't going to be so easy for me to see her and talk with her. Last time we did, we—we disagreed most decidedly and she said I was never to see her again."

"You mean," she asked, "that you had a regular mix-up; but you weren't unkind to Miss Gray?"

"Do you think I would be? No," he went on shaking his head, "I don't think I was ever unkind to Miss Gray; but I should say that Miss Gray was unkind to me. But I don't suppose you know about such things. You've probably never seen her cross."

Pigeon grinned "Oh, but haven't I though!"

"You have—really?"

"You bet I have, Mr. Richard Cameron." She leaned toward him. "Now I'll tell you a secret."

So, sitting there beside the little stream, Pigeon told the strange young man all about

that Saturday morning when the third grade
had trudged to school.

"Say, that was pretty fierce," he exclaimed
when she had finished. "However, she *did* take
your sandwich, and I'm afraid she won't take
mine. I've written her reams and stacks of
letters and she hasn't answered a single one.
Now I ask you, Miss Pigeon Martin, isn't that
a pretty way to treat an old friend? It isn't
playing the game to treat an old friend that
way, do you think?"

Pigeon shook her head. "No, it isn't."

She placed a grubby hand on his arm. "Listen,
I've a plan. I believe I know of a place where
Miss Gray would listen. Nobody could be un-
kind there; it's the loveliest spot to talk in. Miss
Gray loves it dearly; she goes home that way
every day."

"Lead me to it," he cried. "Where is it and
how do I get there?"

"It's our little twisted path through the pines.
Miss Gray says it gives her strength to face Miss
Sallie Foster's back bedroom. I heard her tell
Mother one day." She sprang to her feet.
"I've got to get home if I'm ever going to school
today."

"Never mind," he smiled. "I have a friend
back there who'll take you home in no time."
The nice twinkle had come back to his eyes, and
seizing Pigeon's hand, he hurried her down the

path until they came to the road where waited the most dilapida ed little car imaginable.

"Here's Eliz beth," he told her proudly, "My very good friend. I tell all my troubles to Elizabeth and she tells me hers. Often her troubles are mine also."

"Does she understand what you say?" Pigeon giggled.

"Of course she does." He put his hand on the hood and said politely "Elizabeth, this is Mary Frances Martin, commonly known as Pigeon. This morning while engaged upon a mission of kindness she fell into yonder stream—"

"Halfway," Pigeon interrupted, enjoying herself immensely.

They climbed into the car. The young man did something or other and, with a terrifying noise, off shot Elizabeth racing down the sunshiny road. Pigeon just had time to gasp: "That's our place over there, the white house with the green blinds," before Elizabeth was tearing up the driveway.

"I won't be a second," she called as she scrambled out and up the steps.

Such a rush to bathe and get into fresh things. Mother wasn't at home, so Pigeon chose for herself. She slipped into the new dress with the tiny pink rose buds upon it, put on pink socks and her best patent leather slippers.

The stranger was out of the car and bowing

with his hat over his heart as she came up.
"The Princess Rosebud," he said, gravely. "I
had no idea 'twas a princess in disguise. Your
Royal Highness, I wait your pleasure."

Entranced with his fooling, Pigeon seated
herself and said with dignity "School, please."

"The little path, don't forget that, Your
Highness," he said anxiously.

"We won't," she said, "I'll show you when
we come to it. I hadn't forgotten."

.　　.　　.　　.　　.

"Mary Frances, child, what makes you so
late?" Miss Gray said when Pigeon walked in,
in the middle of a Geography lesson.

Pigeon answered "I had an accident, Miss
Gray. I had to go back home and change my
clothes. Please excuse me."

At recess she called Pigeon to her and asked
what had happened. "Promise me that you
will never go near the place again," she said
when she had heard the story. "Why suppose
you had been hurt and no one there to help!"

It was while the children were on their way
home from school that they passed Elizabeth
parked not far from the place where the little
path left the main road and went winding
among the pines.

It was after dinner and they were all out on
the veranda. The garden was at its loveliest;
filled with a thousand delicate odors, just as if

some mischievous fairy were going about on tip-toe uncorking hundreds of tiny perfume bottles, until the whole garden was drenched in sweetness. The little gate at the end of the rose garden clicked and footsteps could be heard coming up the flagstones; then two figures appeared.

"Here comes Bettina and Bob," their father said.

Right away Pigeon knew that Father was mistaken. It was not her uncle and aunt who were coming toward them through the twilight. She did not need Miss Gray's voice calling, "Are the Martins at home?" to know just who their callers were.

When Miss Gray, in introducing Mr. Cameron, came to Pigeon she smiled and said. "Mary Frances and Richard are friends already, I believe."

"We are indeed," he answered, seating himself on the steps beside her. "Well, Princess Rosebud," he said in a voice intended for her ears alone. "You were right; there was magic in the little path."

That night on the way upstairs to bed Pigeon heard her mother saying to her father: "It looks as if the third grade were about to lose another teacher."

Mother was right. It was not many days before Miss Gray came over to tell them that when school was over, she was going to marry Mr. Richard Cameron, and live in Boston in the red brick house.

"It might never have happened," she told Pigeon's mother, "if it had not been for Mary Frances. We want her to be a bridesmaid. Richard and I both think that the wedding would not be complete without her. Please say she may."

So it was decided that Pigeon was to go to Baltimore in June and stay with Miss Gray's sister until the wedding was over.

Made in U. S. A.